THE PRICE OF FOLLY

All because of twenty-four hours in Paris, and an innocent mistake . . . Rich, handsome, sophisticated Alan Rivers sweeps Paula off her feet. His charming declarations of love and his fervent promises of marriage throw her into a sweet delirium of unreasoning bliss. But when she realises Alan's affections are as false as his promises, and her own feelings are mere infatuation, she soon comes to her senses. Can she free herself from the schemes of the vengeful Alan, and salvage a future with a man who really matters?

DENISE ROBINS

THE PRICE OF FOLLY

Complete and Unabridged

LINFORD
Leicester

First published in Great Britain in 1968

First Linford Edition
published 2016

A catalogue record for this book is available
from the British Library.

ISBN 978–1–4448–2985–3

Published by
F. A. Thorpe (Publishing)
Anstey, Leicestershire

Set by Words & Graphics Ltd.
Anstey, Leicestershire
Printed and bound in Great Britain by
T. J. International Ltd., Padstow, Cornwall

This book is printed on acid-free paper

1

Paula had run away with Alan Rivers.

It is a very big thing for a girl to do; to leave home, parents, friends for the love of a man. She will only do such a thing if she is quite certain that she is madly, desperately, sincerely in love. Paula was certain that she was all those things.

Madly, desperately, sincerely in love with Alan Rivers.

Yet when she stepped out of the train at his side, she was conscious of qualms; of a horrid, uneasy feeling in her heart. Perhaps it was because the journey from London to Paris had been long and tiring, and she felt strange and lost in a strange country; a foreign city. Perhaps because she had never realised until now how infinitely she had trusted Alan in coming with him.

Her pulses jerked, and her heart beat

at a quickening rate; she stood beside him, shivering a little, as she watched him talk to a gesticulating porter, in perfect French (of which she understood and spoke very little), and then walked with him to the taxi, the porter following with her suitcase and Alan's smart leather cabin-trunk.

The man glanced down at her as they walked. It was rather a pale, troubled face he saw, and he frowned.

'Darling,' he said, 'why this silence and depression? The journey's over and here we are in Paris — city of delights, which I'm going to show to you.'

His rich, rather lazy voice had the immediate effect of cheering Paula, who looked quickly up at him, her cheeks colouring, her eyes growing soft and luminous under their thick lashes — golden-brown lashes that curled upwards like a child's.

'I'm a bit tired, Alan,' she answered. 'And — and a bit frightened.'

'Of what?' He smiled tolerantly.

'Oh — of everything,' she said under

2

her breath. 'Don't you realise what this means to me, Alan — running away from home — with you — like this?'

'Oh, yes, of course I know,' he drawled. 'But you counted the cost before you left, and you told me nothing mattered so long as you and I were together.'

'I meant that, and still feel it,' she said gravely. 'But perhaps I shall feel better — more secure in my happiness when we are married.'

He did not answer, but turned from her and gave a curt order to the driver of the taxi.

'4, Rue Delcourt — off the Rue de Rivoli — ' Then to Paula, 'Jump in, darling.'

In the shelter of the taxi, Paula put out her hands to him, with the pathetic gesture of a child who wants comforting.

'Oh, Alan — ' she whispered.

Alan Rivers — at heart a most selfish, calculating man — had the gift of being able to make love to women with the perfection and finish of an artist. He could deceive anybody — let alone a girl as young, as trustful, as romantic as Paula. He was bored with her tremors of fear and had no patience with conscience-stricken fools. Possibly he had no conscience himself. But he took her hands, raised each in turn to his lips — then put an arm about her, hugging her close to his side.

'Such a poor, scared little darling,' he murmured. 'There, kiss me, and tell me you love me.'

Her arms went around his neck. She clung to him, sobbing a little.

'I love you — I adore you, Alan.'

'I adore you, darling,' came his passionate reply. His lips sought hers, crushed them in a long kiss. For a few moments Paula rested, her head thrown back on his shoulder, her eyes closed. She was wonderfully pretty. Her beauty was like wine to him, and had made him lose his head — a very little — when he had first met her, two months ago, in Wilcombe, the dull little village that nestled among the Sussex Downs, within ten miles of Brighton.

Alan Rivers was a philanderer; rich enough to satisfy most of his whims and with no family ties to hinder him, he had been spending a weekend at Brighton. He had driven in his car through Wilcombe on the Sunday morning, and had run over a cocker spaniel belonging to Paula's father. He had stopped to apologise and offer remuneration, and incidentally made himself so popular by his charming manners and personality, that he had stayed at Wilcombe Dean — Paula's home — to lunch. From that moment onward he had wanted Paula — become infatuated with her fresh beauty and innocence. She was one of a large family: old Mr. Broughton was a struggling nurseryman, and Paula divided her time between helping mother with the younger children, and her father with his greenhouses.

Alan remained in Brighton solely for the purpose of motoring daily to

Wilcombe and paying court to Paula. She had soon fallen violently in love with him. But he was not a marrying man, and the first person to discover this was a well-to-do cousin of Paula's who lived in London. This woman had come to Wilcombe; heard of Paula's affair with the handsome, wealthy Mr. Rivers, and warned her and her parents against him. She knew his name — he had a bad reputation — had been twice in the divorce-courts — was notorious for his affairs with pretty women — etc., etc. This resulted in Paula's first quarrel with her parents. She refused to believe a word against Alan. But Mr. Broughton was a man of rigorous habits and morals, and forbade her to see him again.

It was just what Alan wanted. Paula became unhappy, sick of arguments and fights, and all the more determined to go on seeing the man who had taught her such rapture and held out the promise of an existence that might be paradise itself.

She agreed to elope with him.

'Come with me to Paris, and I'll marry you the moment we get there,' he had pleaded.

So Paula had burnt her boats and come; she had regretted the pain she would bring to her parents, but she hated her father for his rudeness to Alan, and his belief in the things her cousin had told him. Alan had denied them and Paula believed in, and staunchly defended, him.

After all, she was going to be Alan's wife. Not for an instant did she doubt his intention to marry her.

Now, in the taxi, snuggling up to him, she felt less afraid.

He smiled at her, lazily ruffled her hair, and told himself how perfect she would look in the chic Parisian clothes he would buy for her. Slim, small, with delicate features and a pale smooth skin that very easily flushed, she was, as he had often told her, like one of the roses her father grew. She had thick bronze hair, naturally curly, and large sparkling eyes.

Alan's pulses quickened as he looked at her.

'You're lovely,' he whispered. 'You don't regret coming with me, do you, Paula?'

'No, no,' she said. 'I adore you, Alan.'

'I'll be good to you,' he said thickly, and he meant it. But his ideas of 'goodness' were not hers.

'Alan, are you sure we can be married at night, in Paris?' she asked in a dreamy voice.

'Oh, yes,' he said easily. 'Don't worry about that. And listen, darling, I'm going to slip this on your finger now, and you can call yourself Mrs. Rivers when we get to my flat, otherwise it'll look strange if I take you there late at night and you are still Miss Broughton.'

She drew away from his arms and sat upright, her cheeks hot, her eyes dark with excitement.

'Yes, I understand, Alan. And then — '

'I'll ring up the registrar, and he'll

come straight round and marry us — I've got the licence,' he said.

Lies flowed from Alan Rivers' mouth. He lied to suit his own ends, regardless of wrecking lives, or breaking hearts. His was that cold, ruthless nature which knows passion, but not love. Paula was a simple, innocent girl brought up in a Sussex village; knowing little of life or the habits and customs of a foreign country. He told her they could be married at any hour of the night in Paris, and she believed him.

She felt thrilled when he slid a slim, platinum circle on her marriage-finger, kissed it, and joked with her.

'There you are, Mrs. Rivers!'

'Oh, Alan!' she said, laughing, starry-eyed. 'It will be wonderful to be your wife.'

She imagined she quite understood his motive in bringing her to Paris for their marriage. Alan had motored her from Wilcombe to Dover in time to catch the afternoon boat. It was just as simple to get married in Paris as to pause en route — in fact, more simple; he had said the registrar would come round to his flat to perform the ceremony. She was so excited, so happy. She did not pause to question the fact that he had the licence; or that an English licence would not be valid in France.

It was thrilling to think Alan possessed a flat in Paris as well as in London. They reached the Rue Delcourt and stopped before a huge white block of flats. Paula stood on the pavement, eagerly looking about her. How lovely Paris seemed on this mild, fragrant night of April. The Rue de Rivoli gleamed with lights, and from the distance came the mellow bells of Notre Dame. All so wonderful — so different — so different from sleepy, tiny Wilcombe.

Yet just a tinge of conscience pricked Paula as she was whirled up in the lift to Alan's flat. She had been naughty to elope with him behind her parents' backs. But she was sure they would forgive her, when she wrote and told them she was Alan's wife.

She forgot home and all connected with it once more, however, when she was in Alan's flat. It was artistic, expensively appointed, and full of interest, for her, since it was to be her future home. And Henri, the Frenchman who managed it, was so nice; had bowed and scraped before her, called her 'Madame' — fully accepted her as his master's wife.

Now she was being taken over the flat by Alan, who had given coat and hat to Henri, and made her take off hers.

After she had inspected the expensively furnished drawing-room, they passed into the bedroom. It was luxuriously appointed, like the rest of the flat. Everything a woman could desire. Paula held her breath in admiration; gave Alan a swift, interrogating look.

'Why, it is all prepared for a woman!' she exclaimed. 'Did you — ?'

'I wired to Henri a week ago and he

prepared it for us,' he lied smoothly.

How was she to know he had always had this luxurious bolt-hole and that Paula was to be only a successor of other women?

The flat was centrally heated, and she felt a trifle oppressed by the warmth, the perfumed sweetness of the atmosphere. It was all so different from her cold, sparsely-furnished home in Wilcombe.

'Different from home, eh, darling?' he murmured, reading her thoughts.

'Very,' she said. 'It all — overwhelms me, Alan!'

She walked with him into the drawing-room again. Her heart beat quickly. With every passing moment she was realising the enormity of the thing she had done in leaving home and coming to Paris with Alan. She twisted the platinum ring on her fingers.

'Alan,' she said in a low voice. 'D — don't leave it too late to send for the — the registrar.'

He put his tongue in his cheek

— then laughed.

'Don't worry, darling. You're tired — so am I. And hungry. Henri has supper waiting for us. After supper we'll — get married, eh?'

She was disappointed. She would so much rather have 'got married' first. She seemed to have lost her appetite. But she did not want to annoy him by insistence. He was so good to her — so wonderful.

After supper, Alan was in a light-hearted mood. He could be sullen, sulky, horrid when displeased, but when he got what he wanted from life, nobody was more charming.

Paula was tired and anxious for the lawful marriage bond between them. But she could not help smiling at him — thinking how handsome he was with his tall, fine figure and sleek, fair head — his pale face with the dark blue eyes that could look so frank, yet hide so much cruelty and intolerance; the well shaped mouth. Paula did not notice the lines of dissipation about those eyes

— the selfish, discontented droop to his lips. Whole-hearted, impulsive, passionate by nature, she had given her love to Alan and trusted him utterly.

Ten o'clock struck, and still Alan had not gone to fetch the registrar. He had drawn Paula down on to the sofa before the fireplace, where Henri had lit a fragrant wood fire, and was playing with her small, slender hands, telling her charming things about her eyes, her hair. She listened to him, fascinated, thrilled, and yet —

'Alan,' at last she dared voice her innermost thoughts, 'isn't it growing late?'

He glanced at his wrist-watch. His pale face twitched slightly. Then with a laugh he caught her in his arms.

'Listen, darling,' he murmured, 'you are as good as married to me — you have your ring — Henri thinks you are my wife — so does the concierge, downstairs, and — '

'Alan!' she broke in, shocked and startled.

He pressed her closer to him.

'Don't look so scared, my baby, I'll marry you tomorrow. We've been talking and it's so late — I honestly believe we have left it too late now.'

'But Alan — ' she struggled to get free, her small face growing very pale — 'you said one could get married at any hour in Paris.'

'I was mistaken,' he mumbled. 'Henri says not after ten. It's a quarter past now.'

'Alan!' she exclaimed. She pushed him back from her. Her eyes were bright with terror. 'You — can't mean it. We must get married tonight!'

'Why not in the morning?'

'I can't stay here, then,' she said, rising from the sofa and pushing his hands away from her. 'I must go — go to a hotel, at once.'

He sprang up — seized her hands — drew her back.

'Nonsense, darling. It's much too late to start scouring for a room. Besides, Henri has unpacked your bag. He thinks we are married. He expects us — '

'Don't go on, Alan!' she broke in. She was trembling. Her lovely eyes looked at him with a horrified, stricken expression.

She was innocent, ignorant, but not a fool. She knew now that Alan had tricked her; that he had never intended to marry her tonight. And she was horribly afraid he had not intended to marry her at all.

'You got me over here under false pretences — you are all that my cousin said of you!' she broke out, in a furious, passionate voice. 'You — '

'Oh, nonsense — don't fly off the handle like that,' he broke in, growing angry himself, because he had expected her to melt into his arms and not fight him like this. 'I'll marry you in the morning, Paula — you know I will.'

'I don't believe you,' she said through tightened lips. 'You have tricked me, Alan.'

'Paula, darling, don't be silly — ' He

caught her in his arms. 'What does it matter — just this one night if we get married tomorrow?'

'Let me go!' she said, her heart beating so fast, so agonisedly, she thought it would break. 'Let me go!'

'Don't you trust me, Paula?'

'No — no — never — again — I can't — let me go!'

'Nonsense,' he repeated, tightening his hold. 'You can't leave me now. Stay, Paula, darling — you won't ever regret it. I swear I'll be good to you — give you anything money can buy.'

She stiffened in his arms. Every word he spoke seemed to fall like a hammer-blow on her heart. She was disillusioned now. She knew exactly where she was — and what he was. Cousin Edith had been right. Father had been right. Alan had made her elope with him, but he had not meant to marry her.

'Let me go, Alan. You have tricked me — insulted me beyond forgiveness. I am not narrow-minded — not a prude

— but, at least, I am not that sort of girl. I can never believe in you or love you again.'

She struggled madly to free herself, to escape from this man who did not love her — who only wanted to ruin her whole life.

Then, suddenly, the stillness of the flat was broken by the sharp clang of the front-door bell.

Alan released her and smoothed back his hair.

'Who the devil is this?' he murmured, his face flushed and annoyed.

Paula's breath came in spasmodic gasps. Her beautiful eyes were wide with fear.

'Oh, I must go — I must get out at once.'

'Stay where you are. Be quiet, you little idiot,' he said in a savage undertone.

She pressed her hands to her breast, feeling dismayed and sick with the pain of disillusionment. She saw him now as he really was, and it was not a pretty sight. The smooth-voiced, charming lover had become an enraged, thwarted brute.

The bell rang again. Alan marched to the door, opened it and listened, as Henri answered the bell. Then he fled back to the girl and seized her arm.

'Listen, Paula, this is an old pal of mine who often turns up at this flat when I'm in Paris. Henri has just told him I am in, and that my wife is here. My wife — d'you understand? What'll he think of you in my flat late at night, and Henri believing us married, if you deny it?'

Paula's heart gave a sick jerk.

'I can't stay — I can't — ' she began.

'Till he's gone,' interrupted Alan in a fierce whisper. 'You must — for your own sake. You'll never see him again after tonight, and once he's gone, you can get away. I won't try to keep you.'

'Very well,' she said through stiff, pale lips.

Her head was whirling, her throat felt dry. But she realised that she was caught — in a horrible position from which she could not now extricate herself. Henri had told the visitor she was Alan's wife. It was true — it was so late — and she was there in the flat with Alan — she must keep up appearances and pretend to be his wife. Afterwards she could and would go.

A slight, rather ascetic-looking man, with a thin, clever face, entered the room.

'So you're in Paris again, Rivers,' he said in an agreeable voice. 'I'm lucky to have found you. I've been here a week and am off to Italy tomorrow. Henri tells me you have your — er — wife with you.'

Alan smiled none too pleasantly. Peter Westbury had been at school with him, he was an intellectual type with a great opinion of himself; a huge sense of right and wrong. He bored Alan to death. But Westbury had money and Alan encouraged all friends of means.

'Come in, my dear boy — nice to see you — just in time for a drink,' he said.

'Yes — my — wife is with me. Peter Westbury, who was at school with me. Westbury — my wife.'

Paula managed somehow to say 'How d'you — do' to Peter — shook hands with him, then dropped limply into a seat and sat silent, trying to compose herself while the two men exchanged commonplaces.

She only vaguely saw Peter's face — he was of no importance to her. But she had seen his gaze travel to her left hand and rest curiously on her marriage-ring — then on her, and felt ready to sink through the floor for shame — shame because she had been forced to act this part of Alan's wife, when she was not his wife nor ever likely to be now.

Peter, whilst chatting with Alan, regarded Paula with his cold, appraising eyes. He was not a lover of women; he avoided them, mistrusted them, and was contemptuous of Alan's preoccupation with pretty faces. He thought this girl extraordinarily pretty. He knew without being told that she was not Alan's wife. Only another of his temporary amours. Peter had little patience with these affairs, but always found Alan an amusing fellow to give him a drink or spin a yarn.

'I wonder how long she's been his 'wife',' he reflected, while he talked to her in a tone of studied politeness. 'Seems a nice enough girl. That childish air is all a pose, I expect — she's not as innocent as she looks. Rivers is a gay dog!'

He stayed half an hour, smoking and drinking with Alan, then departed, telling himself that one day Rivers would get into hot water with these *affaires-de-coeur*.

As soon as he had gone, Paula sprang to her feet and faced Alan, her eyes pools of misery in her small, white face.

'Now I can go — ' she said. 'I daresay you've had enough amusement for this evening. It's very late, and I've got to find a room.'

He argued with her, pleaded, tried in

vain to win back her love and trust, then shrugged his shoulders and let her have her own way.

'Oh, if you're so stubborn, Paula — go!' he said sulkily. 'But I don't know what you're going to do tomorrow. You're a fool not to stay here and have a good time with me.'

'No,' she said, shaking, her head thrown back, 'I should be a fool to do it, and I've been fool enough as it is. You've broken my heart, Alan, and probably you've ruined my life. I shan't dare go home.'

'Oh, hell,' he muttered. 'Stay with me, Paula.'

She took off the platinum wedding-ring — shuddered as she placed it on the table. Then she walked to the bedroom and put on her coat and hat — began to pack her bag. She saw everything through a mist of scalding tears.

He watched her, sullen, red-faced with annoyance. But he made no effort to detain her. He was much too indolent by nature to gain what he wanted by force, if he could not do it by easy methods. Paula was stupid — let her go! He did not care what happened to her. She meant nothing to him.

He tried to give her some money before she left the flat, but she threw it in his face.

'You've insulted me enough,' she said.

'Oh, damn it all, why can't you be sensible and stay with me, Paula?' he muttered. 'You've always said you loved me, and — '

'And now I despise you,' she finished quietly. 'Goodbye,' she said.

She walked down the stairs, and out into the chill of the night air.

★ ★ ★

In the garden of a certain fine old Tudor House known as 'The Whyspers,' near Marlborough, peace seemed to reign with complete supremacy. It was a mild June morning. Under a warm, bright sun, in a cloudless sky, the flowers opened wide their petals. Bed after bed of early roses, of old-fashioned, sweet-smelling herbs surrounded the sloping lawn before the front of the house.

Once 'The Whyspers' had been a monastery. The house still retained one long cloister: and at the end of the garden was the 'Monk's Walk', which the present owner, Sir James and Lady Strange, declared was haunted. A charming old place, it was full of historical interest and always pervaded by a wonderful sense of peace, of repose.

Paula Broughton, sitting sewing in the shade of a tall cedar tree, was conscious of that sense of peace. Yet, even here, in these lovely gardens, she was haunted by the memory of Paris — of Alan, whom she had loved so madly, and who had broken her heart. How could she forget? It was only two short months ago.

Today, somehow, as she sat mending

a skirt belonging to Lady Strange's seventeen-year-old daughter, Geraldine, the memory of her mad infatuation for Alan seemed more vivid, more hateful than ever.

That terrible night, when she had run away from his flat! It was a nightmare. Yet she had come out of it safely — and met with incredible luck. She had wandered miserably through the Paris streets until the early hours of the morning. Finally she had entered a café, which was full of people, and where she imagined she might ask somebody to direct her to decent lodgings for the night. The manager of the café spoke less English than Paula spoke French — grew irritated, and finally ordered her out. Exhausted and terrified, Paula had tried to walk out of the café — then fainted.

An English woman with a party of friends came to her rescue and took her back to her hotel for the night. She kept Paula with her for two days, but after that, was forced to join her husband in

Italy. But, before she went, she gave Paula the name and address of her greatest friend in England — Lady Strange — and wrote to her personally, asking her to help Paula find work, but without telling her Paula's story. That was best buried and forgotten. Paula refused to go back to her own home. They would none of them believe she was still as innocent as when she had left them. She could not face them. She wanted to earn her own living now.

Lady Strange, on receipt of Mrs. Stanhope's letter, and a note from Paula herself, sent for the girl, and took a fancy to her. Gerry was a girl, more sporting than domesticated, and Paula promised to be a quiet and useful girl in the house. So Lady Strange engaged her after their first interview, and Paula came to live at 'The Whyspers', conscious of her good luck.

Her work was light; her surroundings lovely; her employers kind and friendly. But, of course, she felt the complete estrangement from her own family. She had written to her mother, telling her exactly what had happened in Paris, and had received a cold reply from her father. It was as she had expected. She had eloped to Paris with Alan, and they would not accept her version of the details.

'Why so sad, Miss Broughton?' said a cheerful, boyish voice behind her.

She dropped Gerry's skirt and looked round quickly at the speaker. The pallor of her cheeks reddened as she saw the tall, broad-shouldered man smiling at her, swinging a tennis racket in his hand.

'Oh — I — how you startled me, Mr. Strange,' she stammered.

'You shouldn't have nerves at your age,' said Jack Strange. He dropped into an empty chair beside Paula, and pulled out a cigarette case. 'Cigarette?' he smiled.

'No, thank you,' she said, picking up her sewing again.

'You're a very proper girl, Miss Broughton,' he mocked. 'You don't smoke — you don't drink.' He smiled good-naturedly.

Paula's face was hot with embarrassment.

Jack Strange lit his cigarette and watched her while she sewed. He had grown used to seeing Paula at 'The Whyspers' — always a quiet, subdued figure. She seemed afraid to speak to him when he spoke to her; seemed to be always working — or thinking.

'I wish you wouldn't work so hard — you might come and play tennis with me,' he grumbled. 'I've been playing at the net by myself.'

'I'm not here to play tennis, Mr. Strange!' she said swiftly. 'Where is Gerry?'

'Oh, out in the village somewhere. Besides, why shouldn't you play with me? Mother wouldn't eat you!'

She flushed and bent her head lower. Jack Strange's eyes grew tender as he watched her.

'You know I'd like to see more of you than I do. Here am I home on holiday from Ceylon for six months and I want to be amused. Mother has the prettiest girl in the world to live here with Gerry and she won't ever speak to me!'

'Oh, Mr. Strange!' protested Paula. 'I — I'm here to work — not to — to amuse you!'

'Don't be offended,' he begged, leaning near her. 'I didn't mean to annoy you. I — only want to be friends with you, Paula.'

Her eyes softened. His use of her Christian name made her heart-beat suddenly quicken.

'I — oh — it's awfully nice of you,' she faltered. 'But I — Gerry's clothes need a lot of attention — and she — I always seem to have something to do, and — you see, I haven't much time to myself, Mr. Strange.'

'I believe you could if you tried — you ought to dance,' he smiled. 'Were you always so serious?'

'No — not always,' she said.

'I wouldn't mind if you chose to be serious — about me,' he said abruptly.

She gave him a quick, startled look — saw that he was absolutely in earnest. Something between pain and rapture thrilled through her. With sure feminine instinct she realised that Jack Strange was falling in love with her. She liked him tremendously — had liked him ever since his return. His was that frank, youthful sort of nature which appeals to most women. After her experience with Alan Rivers, she found Jack refreshing. He was charming to his mother and sister — a fine sportsman — full of good humour and friendliness. He was given to moods of innocent frivolity which often made her laugh despite herself.

She had been seeing a good deal of him lately — he had followed her about — talked to her — shown an interest which she knew today, beyond doubt, was a serious one. Although it was the last thing in the world she had wanted to happen, she was drawn to him — and realised what a much finer character he was than Alan Rivers. He was only twenty-two, but a man of whom any woman could be proud; could justifiably adore.

Looking at him now, she felt a little thrill of admiration. He was wonderfully good to look at, with his athletic, loose-limbed figure; his fine head, with dark brown hair brushed back from a broad brow; dark, handsome eyes and bronzed, boyish face. Mouth and chin were firm, resolute, courageous. Yet Paula fancied there was passion and sweetness in the curve of those lips. If he loved, Jack Strange would love deeply.

But he was the only son and heir of Sir James. He could not marry a girl out of his own circle. The thing was not to be considered for an instant. Whatever she, personally, felt, she must curb her emotions and cool him off, she reflected. It was her duty. She had heard Gerry speak of Diana Cotesmore — daughter of the M.F.H. who lived on the neighbouring estate. The Stranges all hoped for Jack's ultimate marriage to Diana.

'What are you thinking about, Paula?'

She looked swiftly at the sun-browned, handsome face — then down at her work, conscious that her very ears were burning.

'I — oh, nothing — and — you mustn't call me Paula.'

'But I must!' he said softly.

She could not help laughing.

'I know, but still — '

'Paula, are you afraid of me?' he broke in, and suddenly seized one of the small hands that hovered over Gerry's torn skirt — held it very tightly in a strong, warm clasp. 'Paula, you are beginning to mean much to me,' he added in a low serious voice. 'You are the sweetest, most charming girl I've ever met. Oh, Paula, I like you so much better than the bold, assertive debs — '

'Oh, stop, please!' she broke in, dragging her fingers from his. His face was pale with consternation now. 'Don't say those things to me — please.'

'But I must,' he said, fast losing his head. 'I love you, Paula. I do — honestly. I've been falling in love with you ever since I came home. Paula — darling — when I go back, I want to take you with me — as my wife!'

Sheer astonishment held her dumb for a moment. Her heart beat at an incredible speed. He was asking her to marry him, he, the son and heir of a baronet; and she was penniless, a stupid nonentity who had made a colossal mistake in running away from home.

'Oh, you — you are forgetting who you are — what I am!' she stammered, both hands pressed to her heart.

'No, I'm not. I don't care what our respective positions are. Mother and Dad are not the sort to make a fuss and forbid me to marry you. They will want me to marry the girl I care for. Paula, you must say 'yes'. Darling — you must!'

She did not answer for a moment. But her heart was aching, aching in that moment — yearning for Jack Strange and the love he offered her. She was desperately lonely; had been lonely and unhappy ever since that terrible night in Paris. And Jack could wipe out that bitter memory — Jack's love could make her whole and happy again. She loved him — not as she had loved Alan, with a mad infatuation — but with the real, sincere love that is the foundation of true contentment — real happiness.

She had only to hold out her hand, and he would draw her to him. Yet — how could she take his love and all that he offered, unless she told him about Alan.

'Paula,' he said, his gaze fixed on the beautiful, troubled face, 'there isn't anyone else, is there?'

'No — no — of course not,' she stammered.

'Then you can say 'yes' to me?'

'No — oh, Jack, I can't!' she stammered, her voice broken, her eyes luminous with tears.

He saw the tears and in a moment was on his feet behind her chair, and had wound both arms about her, one hand under her chin, lifting her face towards him. She thrilled as she felt the strength, the secure comfort of his embrace.

'Sweetheart, you can — you must,' he said. 'I love you. You love me, don't you?'

'You know nothing about me!' she breathed.

'I know that Mother's friend sent you to us — met you while you were in Paris, on a holiday. I know who you are — you have told us quite frankly that your father is a nurseryman in Sussex. Well, why not? I'm not a snob and I don't care what position in life you've held so long as you are — just you. And you are everything I most want in the world!'

She listened to his words, agonised. What would Jack say if he knew she had been in Alan's flat in Paris, at midnight — presumed to be his wife?

'But I was tricked — I am innocent,' she mentally argued. 'Why should I tell

Jack about that — risk him doubting me? I love him. I want his love. Why shouldn't I take it?'

He saw the hesitation in her eyes. He drew her closer to him. And suddenly bent his head and pressed a long kiss on her trembling mouth.

That kiss was Paula's undoing. Her eyes closed. Her head sank back on his chest, and her arms went about his neck. She knew that she loved him — that she could no longer say 'No.'

When Jack raised his head again, his handsome face was radiant — his dark eyes passionately tender.

'Oh, Paula — my Paula — I love you,' he said unsteadily.

'I love you, Jack!' she whispered.

He knelt on the grass, and put his arms about her. 'How wonderful — how much too good to be true. No Strange can have been prouder of the woman he means to marry that I am of you, my dearest!'

Those words hurt yet enraptured her. She smoothed the dark, boyish head, her eyes brilliant with unshed tears. Darling Jack! How sweet, how marvellous, his love was to her. But if only she could forget the other man who had insulted and humiliated her — if only she could obliterate the past utterly. But she dared not tell Jack — she was terrified lest he might cease to care, be disillusioned about her. The Stranges had always been proud of their women — she wanted him to be proud of her — could not bear him to imagine unspeakable things about that night in Alan's flat —

A tall girl in slacks and sweater raced across the sun-lit lawn and came upon the amazing sight of Paula in her brother's arms. She stared at them open-mouthed. But Jack turned to her with an outstretched hand.

'Gerry — be the first to congratulate me,' he said. 'Paula is going to be my wife.'

Geraldine Strange stared from her brother to Paula.

'Good lord!' she said, a trifle rudely.

She looked and felt dismayed. She liked Paula, had looked upon her as a nice, quiet little thing who looked after her and did not interfere with her in any way. But as Jack's wife — why, she had never entertained the idea! She and the rest of her family had hoped Jack would marry Diana Cotesmore.

'Wish us luck,' said Jack happily.

Gerry swallowed hard and thrust out a hand to Paula.

'Of course — best of luck,' she mumbled.

Then she turned and fled back to the house to find her mother and impart the astonishing news.

Paula turned to Jack with a quivering laugh.

'I'm afraid she isn't pleased — I'm afraid none of them will be pleased,' she said.

He caught her in his arms.

'Oh, yes, they will. Besides, nothing matters so long as we love each other, darling,' he whispered.

She clung to him.

To say that Sir James and Lady Strange were pleased about their son and heir's proposed marriage would be untrue. Like Gerry, they had thought Paula Broughton a pretty, rather retiring girl with charming manners, and a great help at 'The Whyspers' in a domestic way. But they had neither expected nor wanted Jack to fall in love with her. None of them could accuse her of having led him on or lured him to a proposal, however, and none of them found anything to dislike about her. Violet Stanhope had met her in Paris, looking for a job, and she seemed to come of a decent, respectable family. They could not justifiably forbid Jack to marry her. Besides, Jack was their adored boy, and of an age to choose for himself. Both Sir James and Lady Strange decided that he must do what he wanted.

So they swallowed their disappointment — said farewell to their hopes of welcoming Diana as their daughter-in-law — and were very charming and kind to Paula, who became suddenly of very great importance in the household.

As they sat in the drawing-room after dinner that evening they heard the throbbing of a car outside, and a few minutes later the butler entered, followed by a slightly-built, smartly-groomed man of about thirty.

The instant Paula set eyes on him, her heart gave a leap. She paled. It was Peter Westbury — the man who had seen her in Alan's flat two months ago.

He was greeting Lady Strange with outstretched hands — a smile on his thin, rather austere face, which was painfully familiar to Paula.

'Well, Aunt Clara, are you surprised to see me? I've only just come back from Italy, and driven down here from town. I didn't write you, because I know there's always a bed for me here.'

'Of course, my dear — always,' said Lady Strange, kissing him.

'How are you, Peter?' said Jack in a genial voice. 'Ages since we've set eyes on you. Got a bit of news for you, old chap.'

'Yes, Jack's engaged,' said Gerry.

'Engaged?' repeated Peter. 'Indeed? This is news!'

'My fiancée — Paula Broughton,' said Jack, proudly taking Paula's hand and drawing her forward. 'Paula — my cousin, Peter. Peter's one of the family at 'The Whyspers'.'

He looked full into her eyes. Then he remembered. His face grew hard, his eyes widened. This was the girl he had met as 'Mrs. Rivers,' only two months ago.

During the few seconds in which Peter Westbury stared down into Paula's eyes, she felt transfixed — unable to escape, to speak, to do anything. She could see that Peter recognised her. She suffered agonies while she waited for him to voice his recognition aloud. Only one clear thought remained to her — Jack would know about Alan — would think the worst — and she loved him better than anything or anybody in the world.

Peter was a queer, cold-blooded man with an exaggerated sense of right and wrong. Paula Broughton had done an unforgiveable thing in becoming engaged to Jack, when she was no better than a — but Peter allowed his righteous indignation to carry him no further in thought. Speedily he made up his mind what he would do. He could, of course, denounce her before the family. It was quite clear to him from the pallor of her face and startled, stricken eyes, that she was deceiving Jack — that nobody knew about Paris. On the other hand Peter had a horror of scenes — he considered it bad manners to create a disturbance.

So for the moment he did not show that he had met Paula Broughton before. He smiled at her rather wintrily, then bowed, without attempting to take her hand.

'How d'you do,' he said distantly.

Those brief formal words dragged Paula back from the stupor which had

43

overcome her. She breathed more easily. That Peter knew her she was certain. But he did not intend to denounce her now, at this moment. For that she was supremely thankful. It would give her time to think — to think what best to do and say.

It seemed to her years since he had entered the drawing-room and greeted her; yet his coming had only occupied the space of a few moments. To the others everything had been quite normal. Peter was known to be a reserved man with a rather austere manner. Nobody expected him to greet Paula with warmth.

Paula looked round her, bewildered and afraid. Jack was talking animatedly to his cousin, who had taken a chair, and was lighting a cigarette. Lady Strange sat by Sir James, who had laid aside his evening paper and was listening to Peter's account of his recent travels on the Continent. Gerry, always bored with the home circle, had returned to the novel which she had been reading when her cousin had arrived.

They were all happy, serene, oblivious of the storm in Paula's mind and heart. She envied them their serenity. Suddenly she sat down by Gerry on the sofa, picked up a magazine and stared at the pages with unseeing eyes. All the while she was thinking of Peter Westbury and wondering what he meant to do; what she could do.

It was a cruel trick of fate that he, of all men in the world should be related to the Stranges. She had never heard Jack mention his name, otherwise she might have been prepared for this meeting. She had not dreamed such a thing could be possible. It was a horrible coincidence. Peter was the only person on earth who had seen her in Alan's flat, two months ago. And she had not told Jack — had not dared tell him, least he might suspect her of a wrong she had never committed.

She knew, tonight, beyond all doubt, what Jack meant to her. Her love for

Alan Rivers had been the infatuation of a foolish girl. But her love for Jack Strange was a sincere thing — something amounting to worship.

Raising her eyes she looked across the room at him. He caught her eye and smiled. It was the warm, eloquent smile of a man who is utterly happy and in love. That hint of passion in those dark, fine eyes of his thrilled her. But there could be no happiness for her tonight. Uncertainly, she looked from Jack to Peter. Once more she met that cold, accusing look in which there was both recognition and surprise. She bowed her head, biting her lips to keep herself from crying out aloud.

Why had he come? Oh, why had he come, just when she was beginning to forget Alan and the past — to be happy in the new-found love for Jack Strange?

'Where did you meet your — er — fiancée, Jack?' Peter asked very quietly.

Jack looked away from Paula and smiled frankly and happily at him.

'She came here, a couple of months ago, old man. She's a darling.'

Peter's thin lips twisted slightly.

'You know I never rave about women,' he said.

'Your loss,' said Jack, laughing. 'I've always thought women wonderful. Now that I've met and become engaged to Paula, I think them divine.'

'Moonstruck idiot,' was Peter's mental observation. At the same time his blue eyes regarded Jack with pity. He liked his cousin. Jack was a few years younger and of a totally different temperament. Peter was studious, narrow, reserved. Jack was a sportsman, thoroughly masculine, extravert. One day he would be Sir John Strange — inherit his father's title and estates. Peter was a nephew on Lady Strange's side, but at the same time he considered himself one of the Stranges and was inordinately proud of the good name — of the family reputation.

It was actually a blow to Peter's personal pride to come down to 'The

Whyspers' and find Uncle James' son and heir engaged to Paula Broughton. The fact that she was a sort of superior domestic was bad enough. That she was far from being of blameless reputation seemed horrifying to him.

'You have not told me how she came to get the job here, Jack,' he said to his cousin, eyeing him closely.

'Through a friend of mother's who met Paula in Paris.'

'Ah!' said Peter under his breath. 'I knew I was not mistaken.'

'She was on holiday over there, and wanting a job, when Mrs. Stanhope met her,' added Jack.

Peter smoked in silence for a moment. He wondered what Jack would say when he knew about Paula's 'holiday in Paris'. 'The scheming fraud!' he thought scornfully. She had deceived them all very cleverly. How lucky it was that he had come down to 'The Whyspers' in time to save Jack from making a fool of himself. But Jack had always been romantic, believing in perfect love and divine woman.

Peter's cynical thoughts ran on and on. And all the while Paula sat beside Gerry, wondering how long she would be kept in suspense.

'I can't go to bed without seeing him — speaking a few words to him,' she told herself desperately. 'I can't — '

Gerry yawned and shut her book.

'I'm off to bed,' she announced. 'You coming, Paula?'

'Not just yet,' said Paula gently.

'Well, don't forget you're taking a riding lesson in the morning,' said Gerry. 'And the Cotesmores are coming to lunch.'

'I won't forget,' said Paula, trying to smile naturally. 'I won't lose my beauty sleep.'

She remembered that she had been looking forward to meeting Diana Cotesmore, now that she was Jack's fiancée. She had met her before. Diana had seemed to her very beautiful, spoiled, and wilful. She had been a little afraid of her — especially as she had heard from Gerry that they hoped Jack would marry her. Paula would not have been human had she not felt a thrill of triumph at the thought that she could face Diana Cotesmore tomorrow as Jack's promised wife.

Now the Cotesmores and that little triumph meant nothing to her. She was afraid that at any moment Peter Westbury would accuse her and turn Jack's love into suspicion and contempt.

It seemed to her an agonisingly long time before Sir James and Lady Strange retired. When at last they rose, Jack's mother approached Paula and embraced her quite tenderly.

'Good-night, my dear, and I hope you will always make Jack very happy,' she murmured.

Paula's beautiful eyes filled with tears. She clung a moment, thanking her hesitantly.

'I love him — you know I will always do my best,' she whispered.

2

Paula was left alone with the two men; the one she adored; the one she felt was her bitterest enemy.

She looked at Peter Westbury. His hard, inflexible face did not reassure her. Nervously, she got to her feet.

'I think I'll go to bed and leave you two men to talk,' she said desperately.

'Oh, don't go,' began Jack.

'I'm tired,' she said.

He rose to his feet also. 'Then I'll see you to the foot of the stairs.'

With his delightful laugh, he tucked an arm through hers and walked with her to the door.

Peter's narrowed gaze followed the pair from the room.

'Poor Jack,' he thought with half-contemptuous pity. 'There's a shock awaiting him.'

At the foot of the wide, carved oak

staircase, which was one of the oldest, most attractive parts of the house, Jack took Paula in his arms and bending his smooth dark head, kissed her throat.

'My darling,' he murmured. 'Goodnight — oh, it's marvellous, to know that you belong to me now — that one day you and I will need not to part.'

Acute pain and dread — seemed to engulf her like a flame as she lay against his chest, listening to those whispered words, realising how much she loved this man. For one wild moment she clung to him, both arms about his neck, drawing him closer to her.

'I love you, Jack! Oh, promise me that whatever happens you will always love me!'

'Whatever happens,' he said, nodding. 'How could I help it?'

She shivered a little, but he thought it was with emotion — did not dream it was fear. But she was afraid — horribly afraid of that man in the drawing-room, waiting, no doubt, to shatter Jack's belief in her, to end this dream. And it was grossly unfair and unjust. She was innocent. She was not what he imagined her to be —

'Wait a moment — I'll be back,' she said. 'I left my purse.'

He stood leaning against the bannisters, waiting for her to return, a smile on his lips.

'Wonderful Paula,' he thought. 'How lucky I am.'

Paula fled back to the drawing-room, deserted now save for Peter. Trembling, she stood before him a moment.

'Mr. Westbury — listen,' she said in a low, vibrant voice. 'I know you have recognised me — that it is you who saw me in Alan's flat that night. But I am not what you think — yes, yes, I know I was introduced to you as his wife — but I wasn't — I — oh, I can't explain now. Jack is waiting for me, only — '

'Hadn't you better go back to him?' broke in Peter's hard, cool voice.

'Mr. Westbury, be kind,' she gasped. 'I swear I am absolutely innocent. But give me till tomorrow — let me see you

— speak to you first, before you tell Jack.'

'Why should I do so?'

'Because I implore it,' she said urgently. 'If you have any kindness, any generosity, please let me speak to you tomorrow before you give me away.'

He frowned and tapped the ash from his cigarette. He was neither a kindly nor a generous man. On the other hand he had a sense of justice. He was willing to wait — to see Paula and speak to her — to give her the opportunity to tell Jack the truth.

'Very well,' he said in an undertone, 'I will say nothing tonight.'

'Oh, thank you!' she said, her small hands clenched together. 'Will you be down in the garden, early, please, before breakfast?'

'Very well,' he said shortly.

She turned and fled. She knew Peter would keep his word.

'Found it, darling?' Jack asked her.

'Yes,' she lied.

She loathed even that small lie,

because she loved him — did not want to tell him even the smallest untruth. Yet if he knew about Paris — oh, she dared not tell him that — risk him thinking what Peter so obviously thought.

She felt Jack's arms around her.

'Darling, goodnight — and sleep well!' he whispered as he kissed her.

She clung to him for a moment; then he released her and she went slowly upstairs.

'Soon to be my wife,' was Jack's exultant thought as he watched her go. 'Wonderful to be in love with her.'

★ ★ ★

Morning came.

Paula had not slept at all. Tossing, turning, troubled in her mind, she had not been able to sleep. She felt languid and depressed when she stole down to the garden before breakfast to meet Peter Westbury.

He had kept his promise and risen

early, and stood stiff and silent as Paula approached him, his narrow face rigid and unbending.

'Thank you for giving me this much grace,' was Paula's greeting in a low voice.

'I said I would hear what you had to say,' Peter answered stiffly.

'I only want to tell you — to swear to you that I am absolutely innocent,' she said.

Peter raised his eyebrows.

'That is hard for me to believe — after Paris.'

She reddened. 'Oh, I know appearances are against me. But I swear that I am not — not what you believe me to be. Listen — I will tell you exactly how I came to be in Alan Rivers' flat — '

Quickly, breathlessly, she told her story; told him of her elopement with Alan; of his deception; his promise to marry her, then his attempt to make her remain with him — unmarried.

'He made me keep silence — made me call myself his wife when you arrived that night,' added Paula, twisting and untwisting her hands. 'But I left the flat soon after you did — ran away. It's true — I swear it is true!'

The passionate voice, ringing with sincerity, made Peter frown and hesitate to accuse further. Perhaps she told the truth. He knew that Rivers was an unscrupulous man where women were concerned. And yet — there she had been, in the flat, posing as his wife — and if she had been innocent surely she would not have remained there so late? At any rate it was hard for Peter to credit the fact that any girl in these days could be so ignorant as to believe a man meant to marry her late at night in Paris.

'Don't you believe me?' Paula asked, agonised by the expression on his face. 'Can't you be understanding and give me the benefit of the doubt? I did think Alan meant to marry me — I swear it — and I left his flat — nothing happened. I swear that too — '

Her voice was unsteady. She loathed

the whole conversation — the whole situation.

Peter Westbury dug his hands into his coat pockets.

'Miss Broughton, I honestly do not know whether to believe you or not,' he said. 'Appearances are, I must admit, against you. Rivers was undoubtedly crazy about you and it is difficult for me to believe that he — that you — er — left his flat as you say,' he finished, spreading out his hands with a significant gesture.

Paula bit her lower lip helplessly.

'It is true — oh, I swear it,' she said. 'Mrs. Stanhope — Lady Strange's friend — who looked after me in Paris that night, can prove that she found me in a café after midnight, where I had run away from Alan.'

'Even presuming you did run away that night, what proof have you that you were not with Rivers, as his wife, for some time before that?'

'I only eloped with him that morning.'

'So you say.'

'Oh, how can I make you believe me?' cried Paula in despair. 'Why are you so against me?'

'Because Jack is my first cousin and heir of a fine old family,' he said with hauteur. 'There has never been anything questionable in our family — I do not intend to see Jack make a fool of himself.'

Paula winced.

'I love Jack,' she said in a smothered voice. 'I know I'm not good enough for him — but I love him.'

Peter frowned. Her attitude was that of an innocent woman — a sincere one. Yet he doubted her, hesitated to believe in her, for the family's sake.

'I think you ought to tell Jack about your affair in Paris, anyhow,' he said bluntly. 'Let him decide.'

Paula caught her breath. She went pale.

'I daren't tell him,' she said. 'He might begin to lose faith in me, and that would be grossly unfair. Even if he decided to marry me, in spite of his doubts, I couldn't bear it — couldn't bear there being a shadow between us.'

Despite his own suspicions, Peter admired those words, and his hard eyes softened a trifle as he looked at the girl.

'Look here,' he said curtly. 'I don't want to come between you and Jack if you are innocent — if that affair in Paris was merely the outcome of a stupid infatuation which harmed nobody. But I must have Alan Rivers' word for that. If he corroborates your story — all well and good — your engagement with Jack can stand and I'll say nothing.'

Light sprang to Paula's eyes.

'You mean that? Then I can write to Alan and ask him — '

'I will write and ask him,' broke in Peter with asperity. 'It is to me he must answer. And if he confirms my suspicions, I'm afraid I must ask you to end your engagement with my cousin. You need not tell him the truth. You can just

60

break your engagement quietly and go away.'

Paula shivered there in the sunlight where she stood. She felt cold and wretched. What would Alan say in answer to Peter's questions? Would he be truthful? Defend her? He, more than anyone on earth, knew how utterly ignorant she had been — how unfairly treated that night. Surely he would not be vindictive or malicious — he would do the right thing by her, after all this time?

'If you don't mind, I will go back to the house and write to Rivers at once,' said the implacable voice of Peter Westbury.

'Until his reply comes, nothing more need be said between us.'

Paula bowed her head.

'Thank you,' she said in a low voice. 'And if Alan speaks the truth I have nothing to fear.'

With an almost imperceptible shrug of the shoulders Peter left her.

The rest of that day passed without

event. Paula alternated between happiness — joy in her lover and his love — and despair lest Alan Rivers should ruin her chances of happiness out of sheer spite.

Peter avoided her as much as possible. When forced to speak to her, he was polite. Sir James and Lady Strange were very kind and charming and did everything possible to make Paula feel that they welcomed her and did not resent her engagement to their son.

Gerry's attitude was of half-veiled hostility. She was frankly annoyed by her brother's engagement. She had wanted him to marry Diana.

The Cotesmores lunched at 'The Whyspers' that day. Paula, with all humility, wondered every time she looked at Diana why Jack had not asked her to be his wife. She was beautiful, tall, fair, clever — a brilliant conversationalist — seemed thoroughly at ease with Jack and used her incredibly blue eyes to advantage.

Paula felt dowdy and stupid by comparison. Yet when Jack turned to her, his whole face changed; the friendly look in his dark eyes became one of tenderness, and she realised how much she meant to him — how much more than Diana could ever mean.

Although Diana was perfectly friendly towards Paula, inwardly she seethed with jealousy and dislike of the girl Jack had chosen. Ever since Jack had come back from Ceylon she had been in love with him — had hoped and believed he would one day ask her to marry him. She wanted him, not only because he was good-looking and charming, but because he was the future Sir John Strange. It was a stinging blow to her pride and her hopes that he should have passed her over.

'I won't let Paula Broughton get away with it — I want him myself — ' she thought fiercely.

She would have given much to have known the agonising uncertainty of

Paula's position as Jack's future wife — to have known what lay in Peter Westbury's mind.

Meanwhile, Paula suffered and waited — happy only when she was alone with her Jack, close in his arms, where she felt safe and protected.

At the end of the week her suspense over Alan's answer was ended — but in a manner calculated to send her yet further into the depths of despair.

Peter found her alone in the library, reading, one evening just before dinner. The others had not yet come down. She sprang to her feet when he entered the room, an opened letter in his hand.

'You — you have heard from — Alan?' she stammered.

'Yes,' he said, 'I have. He makes no statement — does not answer any of my questions. But he says he has been looking for you for weeks and is coming over from Paris immediately, straight to this address. This letter was written two days ago. That means he may be here at any moment.'

Paula, dismayed, put a trembling hand to her lips.

'No, no — he mustn't come here! Mr. Westbury, you can't — you won't let him come — surely?'

Peter was quite unmoved. Alan's evasive letter had more or less convinced him of this girl's guilt. He looked into Paula's terrified eyes, his own like cold, blue stones.

'Why shouldn't I let him come?' he asked contemptuously. He could scarcely have been more insulting.

But Paula was beyond being proud just at this moment, and beyond caring whether Peter insulted her or otherwise. She was literally panic-stricken at the idea of Alan coming to 'The Whyspers' to destroy her happiness — to break Jack's heart and her own.

With a feverish gesture she caught Peter's arm with both hands.

'No, no — please, please stop him!' she implored. 'Mr. Westbury, I'm not guilty of — of what you think. Oh, I swear it! But Alan can't come here now

— it — it would be an impossible situation!'

'It should never have been allowed to become impossible,' said Peter, drawing his arm from her with a movement that stung Paula even in her terror and anguish. 'You had no right to accept Jack's proposal in the first place, knowing that you were Alan's — '

'No, no!' she interrupted, refusing to let him utter the word which she did not in any way deserve. 'You have no right to say that — to believe such a thing against me.'

'I tried not to believe it after our conversation the other morning,' he said. 'I decided to let Rivers himself settle the matter for good and all. I wrote to him. I have told you his answer. He refused to answer my questions concerning your presence as his wife in his flat that night, and announced his intention of coming straight down to Wiltshire to see you personally. Now I can and will do no more for you.'

Paula stumbled to the nearest chair, sat down and leaned her head against a cushion, gasping a little for breath.

'Mr. Westbury,' she said, 'I can only assure you that I am innocent. I've said that so many times and you won't believe me — ' her voice broke pathetically, 'but I swear it to you on my most sacred oath.'

'Then why didn't Rivers admit it — leave you alone?'

'I don't know,' she said in a hollow tone. 'I can only suppose he has some ulterior motive in wanting to come here.'

'Of course,' said Peter slowly, 'he may be coming personally to assure me of your — er — innocence.'

'Yes, yes, it may be the answer,' she said hopefully. 'Oh, it is that, of course. It must be. He knows I was not to blame for — that night in Paris.'

'In which case, of course, I shall be ready and willing to apologise to you,' added Peter, his voice and manner as chilly, as distant as ever.

Paula drew a slender hand across her brow.

'I won't want you to apologise,' she said in a low tone. 'I realise you have had cause to be suspicious. I only want peace — and the right to enjoy my happiness with the man I truly love.'

'At any rate, whether you are innocent or guilty, I am afraid I cannot prevent Rivers coming here if he wishes to see you,' Peter went on. 'He will have to be introduced to the family as an old friend of mine — and yours.'

'He is no friend of mine,' whispered Paula. 'I never want to see him again. I loathe the memory of him.'

Peter shrugged his shoulders.

'I am sorry. But if he comes it cannot be helped.'

'Unless he has some particular wish to harm me, he will tell you the truth,' said Paula. 'Then perhaps you will leave me alone — all of you.'

Peter reddened. Somehow Paula made him feel ashamed of himself, and he resented the feeling. He was about to make some sharp remark when the library door opened and Jack came in — bouyant, youthful, very smart in his well-cut dinner jacket.

'Hullo, Paula, darling! Hullo, Peter — how's everything?' he said cheerfully.

He always came into a room like a strong, fresh breeze, bringing with him an atmosphere of happiness that seemed the essence of perfection to Paula. She adored him — and this was the man whom Peter and Alan between them wanted to take from her.

He was at her side before she had time to rise and greet him, sitting on the edge of her chair, putting an arm around her shoulders.

'Sweetheart, you look pale. Not ill, are you?' he said, a note of concern in his deep voice.

A sudden wave of passionate resentment against Peter for hurting and terrifying her swept over Paula. She was innocent. Why should she suffer as though she were guilty? Even if Alan came, he must surely vindicate her. She had nothing to fear — her conscience was clear. Colour returned to her sensitive face and she flung back her head, looking with defiant, brilliant eyes at Peter.

'No, I'm not ill, Jack, darling,' she said in aloud, clear voice. 'Nothing wrong with me. I've just been having a — a sort of political argument with Mr. Westbury.'

'Peter likes an argument, don't you?' laughed Jack, looking at his cousin humorously. 'And what do you think of Paula's powers of reasoning? I can't argue with her for long. She's far more intelligent than I am.'

'Oh, my dear!' murmured Paula, leaning against him with a deep sigh which was stifled against his sleeve.

Peter, who hated any kind of display in public, turned his back on the pair and moved towards the library door.

'Oh — most intelligent — very clever, I should say,' he remarked.

The sneer in that observation was lost upon Jack, but Paula winced. When the door closed on Peter, she turned with a little gesture of abandon, flinging her arms about his neck.

'Jack, Jack, I love you so!' she said in a smothered voice. 'Oh, darling, I'd die if your love was taken from me now.'

His handsome, laughing face grew serious at once. He drew her into his arms, bending to kiss her.

'Baby, why should my love be taken from you? It can't be, when I adore you and worship you!'

Her eyes, clouded with grief, looked beyond him to the closed door through which Peter Westbury had just passed.

'No, perhaps not,' she said. 'But sometimes I am afraid — '

'You need never be afraid of that. I shall love you all my life, Paula,' said Jack in an earnest voice.

She clung to him speechlessly for a few moments. She would have given half her life to be as happy, as peaceful in her mind as he was, to be able to obliterate that affair with Alan, which had been so innocent, yet for which she was paying such a bitter price.

The library door burst open. Gerry came in — saw them in each other's arms — and marched out again, banging the door behind her.

Lady Strange, crossing the lounge, was nearly knocked over by her tall, youthful daughter; reproached her, then noted the look of disgust on her face.

'What's the matter, my dear?' she said, smiling.

Gerry hunched her shoulders and nodded in the direction of the library.

'Jack and his Paula are in there,' she said. 'It makes me sick to think that Jack should be making such a fool of himself over that girl. Why couldn't he have married Diana?'

'My dear!' protested Lady Strange, and her beautiful face was pained. 'You really must try to think more kindly of Jack's engagement. We are all — er — disappointed about Diana — but we are trying to welcome Paula with open minds and hearts, and you must do the same.'

'M'm,' said Gerry, scowling. 'Well, we none of us know anything about Paula's people or past, remember, mother.'

Lady Strange went into the library, her gentle heart and generous mind considerably troubled by her young daughter's words.

Somehow she did wish they knew a little more about Paula.

★   ★   ★

Paula did not see Jack alone again that evening. Dinner over, Diana Cotesmore arrived, and soon afterwards the Whites from a large house in Marlborough — great friends of both the Stranges and Cotesmores. They had only been married a year and were devoted to each other. Paula thought them a charming couple. Delia White was a beautiful woman of thirty. Major White — a huge, fair man with twinkling blue eyes and a great sense of humour — was retired from the Army and had at one period of the war been Jack's battery commander.

Neither Hugh White nor his wife seemed able to enjoy life separated for more than a few moments at a time. Paula watched them with a tremendous feeling of envy. How happy they were — adoring each other — husband and wife.

'The Whites are a good pair — as old-fashioned in their love for each other as they can be,' Jack had whispered to Paula earlier in the evening. 'We will be like that when we're married, won't we?'

Paula had smiled and nodded, thrilled by the warm look in Jack's eyes. But later, while she sat beside Lady Strange watching Jack dance with Diana Cotesmore, and Hugh White quite unfashionably enjoy a samba with his pretty, dark wife, she felt strangely depressed and anxious.

When they were married — if only they were married now — if only she could feel as confident of the happy future as Jack —

A sharp little pang of quite unreasoning jealousy hurt Paula tonight while her eyes followed Jack and Diana round the softly-lit room. Paula thought how beautiful Diana looked tonight — almost as tall as Jack — exquisitely made, and like an exotic flower in a magnificent dress of blue organza that sparkled and scintillated as she moved.

With some bitterness Paula looked down at her simple black lace gown.

'Why aren't I brilliant, proud, beautiful — like Diana?' she inwardly cried. 'She is far more suited to Jack than I am. Yet I love him so — oh, I don't want to lose him now!'

Jack, in the highest of spirits, finished dancing with Diana, then piloted her out into the moonlit garden for a breath of air. He would far rather have been out here with Paula, but seeing that she was about to dance with Hugh, took Diana for a walk instead.

'Awfully hot in that room tonight,' he remarked as he walked down the path mopping his face.

'Yes — much too warm,' Diana agreed.

Her heart was beating fast. She had been strung up to a pitch of emotion, of which Jack was entirely unconscious, by her dance with him. He did not know that the pressure of his arm — his good looks — had fired her to an almost crazy passion for him tonight; that she hated Paula Broughton with all her heart and soul; that she wanted him more than anything or anybody on earth.

She looked just a calm, self-possessed young woman, with an independent air; but in reality she was primitive woman — in love — fiercely determined to win her man. The flower-scented garden, the moonlight, the romantic hour, all went to her head as she walked down the garden path at Jack's side.

'It's good to have you to myself, Jack,' she said, trying to speak lightly. 'I hardly ever see anything of you these days and we used to be such friends before you went to Ceylon.'

Quite oblivious of her consuming passion for him, Jack turned to her with his frank, friendly smile.

'We did, and still are, I hope, Di,' he said.

'Oh, of course,' she murmured, 'but now you are engaged — ' she finished with an expressive shrug of the shoulders.

'My engagement to Paula doesn't spoil my friendship with you or anybody else,' he observed. 'Paula isn't like that — she would hate me to give up my friends because of her, bless her.'

His tender tone when speaking of Paula made Diana clench her hands.

'Let's sit down here a moment and have a cigarette, shall we?' Jack went on as they came to a rustic seat at the end of the rose-walk.

She tried to conquer the rising emotion in her and sat down by him. It was a charming part of the garden, hidden from the house by tall firs. Just in front of the seat a marble faun, with a grinning, enigmatical face, stood on a square piece of lawn. The statue looked lifelike in the clear, pale moonlight. Jack regarded it with humorous eyes.

'I remember playing round that faun when I was a boy,' he murmured as he lit a cigarette for Diana. 'Cunning-looking beast, isn't he?'

His banal, cool chatter maddened the girl who was filled with passion for him — with an almost savage desire to win him away from Paula Broughton. The slender, manicured fingers holding her cigarette were not quite steady.

'Yes,' she said, 'isn't he?' Then: 'Jack — I suppose you are very happy about your engagement?'

He turned surprised brown eyes upon her.

'Of course, Diana. Tremendously.'

She swallowed hard. The colour had left her cheeks. He noticed suddenly how pale and distressed she looked — and how beautiful, with the moon-light on her golden head.

'Why, Diana — what's the matter?'

he asked kindly. 'Anything wrong, my dear? Are you in any difficulty? You can confide in me, you know!'

Oh, how he infuriated and tormented her! She flung her cigarette away with a savage gesture.

'Yes — I am rather,' she breathed. 'But I can't confide in you, Jack.'

He was a man madly in love. And like so many men in love, easily jumped to the conclusion that others around him were in love. Perhaps Diana Cotesmore had lost her heart to someone who did not return her affection, he thought compassionately. He was sorry, if it was the case — and astonished. She was such an attractive girl.

'Why can't you confide in me?' he asked. 'I never dreamed you had any sort of trouble. Tell me all about it, and if I can do anything — '

'You could do everything!' she finished in a tense voice. 'But I can't confide in you, Jack. You would despise me — never understand — what your engagement meant to me. Oh, what am I saying? I must be mad!' she added, breaking off with a dramatic gesture, an added vibrancy in her voice. (Diana Cotesmore was a consummate actress.)

She covered her face with both her hands. And Jack Strange stared at her bent golden head, his good-looking face pale and serious, his fine dark eyes very distressed — and surprised. For, of course, he could not fail to realise what she meant — what her broken, wild words implied. It was almost a shock to him to know that Diana was in love — with him — that she suffered on account of his love for Paula. He would not have been human had he not been a little flattered by what she had revealed, but at the same time he was horribly embarrassed and sorry for her. He hated to see a woman suffer. He had always thought of Diana as a cool, self-possessed young woman, therefore generously allowed that she must have lost her head slightly tonight.

Awkwardly he touched that bowed, beautiful head.

'Di — my dear — I'm so sorry — but I — don't know that I understand,' he stammered kindly.

She knew that he did. But she took her cue from him. Raising her head she looked at him; tears on her thick lashes and sparkling very effectively in her brilliant blue eyes.

'No, no, of course not; let us go back. I — I'm being a fool. Give me a cigarette,' she said hurriedly.

Gladly enough he lit a cigarette for her. He was rather silent as he walked back with her to the house. But she had done all that she had intended to do — let him guess she was in love with him, and she knew he would not forget it. What man could? Despite his honest love for Paula, he might remember Diana at some future date when he needed consolation. Diana was a clever girl — content to wait the auspicious moment.

Just before they reached the house,

Diana paused and held out a hand. Her face was delicate, tear-stained, appealing.

'I — I'm just going to wander for a walk by myself. I'll be in in a moment. Don't take any notice of me, Jack.'

He took the hand in a firm grip. He felt so sorry for her. Though had he known what scheming thoughts lay behind that smooth forehead, what passionate dislike and jealousy of Paula, he would have loathed her.

'Always remember I'm your friend, Di,' he said kindly.

She turned from him and walked away down the path towards the drive, which led out on to the main road to Marlborough.

She had done her work for this evening. Now she wanted to be alone; to remove the traces of tears from her cheeks and go back to the ballroom looking carefree and radiant. Jack would not forget what she had revealed, and he would be intrigued and baffled by her seeming gaiety. Oh, yes, Diana was cunning — and she was all out now to win from Paula the man she desired.

As she approached the entrance to the drive, she was suddenly half-blinded by two dazzling headlamps from an approaching car. She sprang to one side of the roadway, and the lights were thrown full upon her, showing up her tall, fine figure in the blue and silvery gown. The car stopped and the driver got out and approached her, raising his cap.

'Pardon me, but is this 'The Whyspers'?' he asked in a charming, well-bred voice.

Diana saw by the light of the headlamps that the stranger was tall, good-looking and smartly dressed.

'Yes. These are the gardens of 'The Whyspers'.'

'Oh, thanks very much,' said the man. 'I've come to see a Miss — er — Broughton.'

Diana pricked up her ears. Jack's fiancée! Was this man a relation of Paula's, or an old admirer?

'Miss Broughton lives here too, yes,' she nodded. 'The whole family are up at the house dancing. I am Miss Cotesmore — a guest here. I just came out for some fresh air. It's such a wonderful evening, isn't it?'

'Marvellous,' he murmured, putting his cap back on his sleek fair head. 'Allow me to drive you back to the house.'

Diana smiled slowly and decided to take the offer. She seated herself in the car, and the man took his place at the wheel.

'May I introduce myself, Miss Cotesmore?' he said. 'My name is Rivers — Alan Rivers.'

Diana made a mental note of the name.

'And you are a great friend of Miss Broughton?' she asked sweetly.

'Quite an old friend,' said Alan with his tongue in his cheek. 'Do you know Paula well?'

'She is engaged to my oldest friend — Jack Strange,' said Diana, watching him covertly from beneath her long lashes.

'Ah!' said Alan, and she saw his eyes narrow.

'A delightful couple,' purred Diana.

'When I heard about it it was a distinct shock to me,' said Alan.

'Indeed?' said Diana very eagerly.

There was no time for further conversation between these two, who were equal in their capacity for cold, cruel selfishness. They had arrived at the house. But Diana had learned a great deal in a few seconds. She had already gathered that this Alan Rivers was an old suitor of Paula's. So far, so good, and now to make Jack jealous.

'Come straight in,' she said to Alan. 'I will take you to Paula.'

'She may not expect me,' murmured Alan, divesting himself of his coat, which he hung up in the hall. 'I drove down and just had time to put my stuff at the Royal George in Marlborough, and dash out here after a hurried dinner, to see her for a few moments. I hope Sir James and Lady Strange won't mind — '

'I'm sure they'll be delighted to welcome a friend of Paula's,' said Diana, secretly enjoying herself. For she knew in her heart of hearts that in all probability Paula would not want to see this man at all.

Deliberately she piloted Alan into the drawing-room without giving Paula warning, and led him up to Paula, who was standing with Jack, laughing up at him. As she saw the hatefully familiar figure of the tall, fair man who walked into the drawing-room beside Diana, the laughter left her face and her eyes went dark; her cheeks ashen.

'A surprise for you, Paula,' said Diana in her sweetest voice. 'An old friend of yours — Mr. Rivers — to see you!'

Alan's eyes met those of the girl whose heart he had nearly broken — whose life he had tried to ruin — and he smiled, a slow, meaning smile that terrified her, chilled her.

'My dear Paula,' he said in a theatrical voice, holding out both his hands. 'How wonderful to see you again — at last!'

3

Paula wished in that moment that the floor would open and swallow her up. She stood there, staring at Alan, quite conscious that everybody else in the room was gazing in their direction. She could almost feel Jack's surprised, questioning glance, although she dared not meet it.

Alan seemed quite cool, quite happy.

'Simply wonderful to see you again,' he repeated, both hands still extended.

Paula pulled herself together with an enormous effort. Aware that she was being stared at because she made no movement or sound, and that she must break the silence that had fallen over the little assembly in the drawing-room since Alan's entrance, she put out one trembling hand and endeavoured to greet him composedly.

'I — what a — a surprise! — er

— how do you do?' she stammered.

Diana Cotesmore had been watching her. 'It's perfectly obvious she's taken aback by the appearance of this Mr. Rivers, and that she didn't want to see him,' was her mental observation — drawn with great secret satisfaction. 'So far, so good. I must keep an eye on dear Paula. I'm not at all sure she's the little angel Jack imagines!'

Alan took Paula's hand and pressed it warmly. He was quite aware that she did not wish him to show such warmth in public, but he ignored the silent appeal in her eyes deliberately, enjoying her discomfiture. She had escaped from him in Paris on a night when he had wanted her wildly. He was going to punish her for that night.

'Dear Paula,' he murmured. 'Just the same! You haven't altered a bit. More beautiful than ever, perhaps!' He kissed her hand.

Lady Strange, regarding him from the other side of the room, pursed her lips and turned to Sir James.

'I don't think I like this young man, James,' she murmured. 'And he appears to be an old friend of Paula's from the way he speaks.'

Jack looked quickly at the tall, sleek-headed man who was greeting his fiancée in such a familiar fashion, then at Paula. He had not the slightest idea who the newcomer was, and was not at all sure he liked the way he spoke to Paula. But if he were a friend of hers that was sufficient for Jack, who loved and trusted her implicitly.

'Do introduce me to your friend, darling,' he murmured, putting an arm about her shoulders.

The frozen look of fear, or repugnance, was still in Paula's beautiful eyes. The sight of Alan, the touch of his lips on her hand had shivered her with a thousand memories — memories of a past she had tried so hard to forget, but which now came sweeping back upon her, almost choking her. She knew now how utterly unworthy he had been of her childish adoration, and how much she loathed and despised him today. She would willingly have turned her back on him, thrown herself into the arms of Jack — begged him to take her away where she could never see that handsome, deceitful face again. But here she was in a drawing-room full of people who were watching her; forced to do the conventional thing and welcome the man who had dared to force himself upon her in this fashion. And she was utterly in his power, because she had not told Jack about that one regrettable incident in her past.

The room seemed suddenly to be hot and stifling. Suffocated, she put a hand up to her brow. In another moment she feared she would faint.

'This is ghastly,' she thought. 'I must pull myself together — '

'Paula, dearest, are you all right?' she heard Jack's anxious voice, and, turning, looked into the brown eyes which could thrill her so completely. But she felt no thrill in that instant — only

91

terrible, aching regret that Alan Rivers had once, by trickery only, occupied his place.

She smiled — a smile that would have wrung Jack's heart could he have guessed the effort it cost her.

'Quite well, thank you, Jack — only the room is — so warm. Yes, of course — let me introduce — an old friend of mine. Mr. Alan Rivers.'

'How do you do?' said Jack courteously, holding out a hand. 'Any friend of Paula's is welcome to 'The Whyspers'.'

'My fiancé — Mr. Strange,' added Paula, turning her eyes upon Alan.

Alan looked down into those exquisite eyes that had once fascinated him, and which still seemed to him particularly alluring. He read all the agony of appeal in her gaze. She was engaged to this man Strange, and obviously wished him, Alan, to keep silent about Paris. He was not so sure he wanted to keep quiet. But for the moment he could not very well cause an upheaval, he reflected. So he shook Jack's hand warmly.

'Very glad to meet you,' he murmured. 'Hope you don't mind me crashing in at such a late hour, but I only arrived in Marlborough this evening, and felt I must come and call on Paula before the night ended.'

'Delighted you came,' said Jack in the same courteous fashion. Then to Paula: 'Introduce your friend to my parents, sweetheart.'

She did so, moving, speaking now like an automaton, and feeling ice-cold. Only her head burned — throbbed — with the pain of her fear and despair. She hated having to introduce Alan to Jack's parents — to the Whites — to Diana Cotesmore, who had met him outside, apparently, and brought him in. In desperation she turned to Peter Westbury, who must know the torment in her mind.

'Please talk to him — tell him to go away,' she said in an undertone. 'You know him — you can send him away

— I'll see him tomorrow — but not before all these people — I implore you — '

'Very well,' said Peter, taking care that nobody heard him. 'I'll see to it.'

She turned away from him, grateful beyond words. But Peter did not comply with her request because he pitied her. He did not understand that her anguish and terror were born of her fear of losing Jack, because she loved him so much. Her pale, stricken face and desperate eyes were all evidences of her guilt, to Peter. But maintaining his dislike of scenes in public, he saved the situation for Paula.

'Fancy meeting you here, Rivers!' he exclaimed as he shook hands with Alan.

'Well, Peter, how are you?' said Alan brightly.

'Do you two know each other?' asked Jack in rather a relieved voice.

'We were at school together,' said Alan.

'Mr. Rivers is an old friend of Peter's — isn't that strange?' murmured Jack's mother, rather more happily, to Diana.

'M'm,' murmured Miss Cotesmore, not at all sure she was pleased about this. It made things look so much better for Paula. But she was quite confident from the way Paula had looked and acted when Alan Rivers had first entered the room, that there was something between them, and she meant to unearth it before she relinquished all hopes of winning Jack for herself.

Jack was frankly glad to find the newcomer acquainted for so many years with his cousin. He could not honestly say he liked the look of Alan Rivers. The man was smooth enough, but rather the typical ladies' man, for whom Jack had no use.

Paula breathed more easily, and a little colour came back to her cheeks as she stood there watching Peter and Alan talk.

'Look here, Rivers,' Peter was saying as he exchanged cigarettes with Alan, 'I think it's rather odd behaviour to call upon Miss Broughton in this fashion. I suppose you have some definite reply to make to my letter, but I'd rather you came round in the morning to see her and me. This is hardly the moment — '

'No, no, of course not,' finished Alan easily, lighting his cigarette. 'I've no intention of making any scene. I've come, as you say, to reply definitely to your letter. Devil of a business this. Who'd have dreamed Paula would have come here and got herself engaged to your cousin?'

'It is all very awkward, and I wish to goodness it had not happened,' said Peter angrily. 'I have drawn only one conclusion from what I saw that night I visited you in Paris, and — ' he finished with a significant shrug of the shoulders.

Alan's brain worked quickly. He saw exactly what had happened. He was greatly surprised to think that Paula and Peter should have come across each other again in this extraordinary fashion. He had not dreamed they would ever meet again after that night. And he saw too that Peter could only imagine one thing, since Paula had been introduced to him as 'Mrs. Rivers.' Now she was in love with this fellow Strange and meant to marry him, and Peter, standard-bearer, so to speak, of the Strange family, would not permit such a marriage unless he was assured of Paula's innocence.

Alan's dark blue eyes narrowed slightly and rested upon Paula. He had not seen her for months, but he had been haunted by the memory of her — had regretted allowing her to escape him. He had never seen another girl quite so attractive to him — quite so sweet. He had tried to forget her, to console himself with others, but had failed. He had come to the conclusion that he wanted Paula Broughton and no other woman, and that if he could not possess her any other way, he would even go the length of marrying her.

Now, to find her engaged to another man and in love with that man; to meet coldness, repulsion from her, only fired him to greater longing for her. He had come dashing down to Wiltshire in answer to Westbury's letter, determined to put an end to Paula's new love-affair and make her return to him.

'I won't stay more than a few moments now,' he whispered to Peter. 'I'll just have a word with Paula, then be off. I'll get her to meet me in the morning.'

'Very well,' said Peter coldly.

Alan moved to Paula's side. She was very remote as she stood before him. Nobody else was within earshot now. The others were dancing again.

'Why have you come?' she asked stiffly.

'To see you, my dear,' he answered.

'What's the idea? When I left you in Paris, I left for good. I never meant you to see me again.'

'But I meant that you should,' he said softly, looking down into her face. 'Paula, believe me, I haven't known an hour's peace since you went.'

'You deserve no peace,' she said in a low, agitated voice. 'Oh, how dare you come here like this — introduce yourself to my future husband — his relations — his friends — ' She broke off, too agitated to continue.

And the man who had once loved her superficially realised in this moment that he wanted her now more than anything. His eyes glittered calculatingly. When Alan Rivers really wanted a thing he cleverly concealed the fact and turned the thought over and over in his cool, scheming brain.

'Don't waste time and words reproaching me, my dear Paula,' he said lightly. 'I have come to see you for very good reasons, and as for your future husband, well — '

'Well, what?' She held her body tense.

'We will discuss that tomorrow,' said Alan meaningly. 'The music is stopping and Jack will be coming to claim you in a second. Listen, Paula — tomorrow morning at eleven o'clock — at the

'Wheatsheaf' — half a mile from here, between this house and Marlborough — you know it? Meet me there.'

'No,' began Paula in a fierce undertone.

But he interrupted.

'Yes,' he said masterfully. 'You can't refuse. And if you are not there, Paula — so much the worse.'

He moved from her side to Peter, and simultaneously Jack, who had finished his dance with Delia White, hurried across the room to Paula, eager to be with her for a few moments.

'Come out for a breath of fresh air in the garden, sweetheart,' he whispered.

She went with him, feeling cold and sick with fear. Alan's threat — 'so much the worse' — had terrified her. Why was he behaving in this strange, over-bearing manner — forcing her to meet him against her will?

'Isn't he going to tell the truth?' she thought, a deadly sensation of despair enveloping her.

In the fragrant hush of the garden

Jack Strange put an arm around the girl he worshipped and looked down at her face — pale in the moonlight. He did not read the terror and anguish that lay in those beautiful eyes. He only thought how exquisite she was.

'My darling, Paula,' he said in a low, passionate voice. 'I've wanted you so much! It was boring having to dance with Diana and Mrs. White and leave you to other men. I'd far rather have danced with you — just you — the whole evening. Oh, Paula, I think I shall carry you off tomorrow and marry you — elope with you — I want you so much!'

She buried her face against his shoulder, trying to restrain the tears that threatened to come. 'Jack, oh, Jack, hold me closer — closer — never let me go!'

'I will never let you go, my baby,' he said, tightening his clasp on her. 'You are my whole world now. If it were not that mother and dad will want a conventional wedding, I'd elope with

101

you tomorrow — but I can't — for their sakes — we must do the thing properly — ' He broke off with a youthful, embarrassed laugh.

She nodded. She knew and understood so well — could picture the conventional wedding Lady Strange would glory in and which they would both hate. At the same time, she wished passionately that Jack could indeed carry her off tomorrow and marry her. She was desperately afraid — afraid of Alan Rivers and Peter Westbury, who seemed in league against her. And she dared not tell Jack the story of Alan and Paris — in case he did not believe the truth. He called her his 'whole world' — he believed in her complete innocence and truthfulness. It would break his heart as well as hers if things went wrong, and he began to wonder.

What would tomorrow bring? What would Alan have to say? She would have to go to the 'Wheatsheaf' and speak to him — implore him to go away and leave her alone — in peace with the man she loved.

She looked up at Jack's strong face; wondered in sick grief how she could ever have cared for Alan — wished with an even keener grief that she had met and fallen for Jack first.

Jack caressed the head that just reached his chin.

'Now, sweetheart, tell me about this fellow who was at school with Peter. I've been aching to ask you about him. Felt quite jealous,' he laughed.

'You need not be,' said Paula, half closing her eyes. 'I — I don't particularly like Mr. Rivers.'

'Aha! Disappointed suitor — pursuing Paula and a bit sick because he finds her engaged to me, eh?' said Jack. 'That's it, isn't it?'

She murmured a reply in the affirmative. The subject of Alan distracted her, and she did not want to lie to Jack more than was strictly necessary. At any rate, Jack was convinced in his mind that Rivers was a disappointed suitor who had met her in the past and was annoyed by her engagement.

'I could never really be jealous of you, Paula,' Jack said after a pause. 'I trust you implicitly.'

She crimsoned uncomfortably.

'I trust you,' she said in a stifled, small voice.

'I've never loved any woman but you,' he said.

'If only I could tell him I'd never loved any man but him!' thought Paula bitterly.

Jack was thinking of Diana — poor Diana, who had lost her head tonight and shown that she cared for him. Somehow the thought of Diana only intensified his love for Paula. He looked deep into her eyes.

'We must go back to the others,' he whispered. 'But one more kiss before we go — and tell me again that you love me, darling.'

★ ★ ★

Paula slept little that night; she remained in a state of inner turmoil, chafing against the necessity for obeying Alan and meeting him next morning.

It would mean deceiving Jack — how could she tell him she was going alone to meet Alan Rivers? It would immediately make him suspicious. She loathed telling him an untruth — hated the morass of deceit into which she was slowly but surely being drawn. And it was not her fault — she knew she was innocent of wrong — that she was paying the price of a sin she had never committed, because the man she had trusted had betrayed her trust. Appearances were armed against her.

When the morning came, she managed to excuse herself from the family circle and make her way out to the 'Wheatsheaf' alone. Jack had, of course, wanted to come with her, but she had hinted that she wanted to shop in the village by herself and buy something for him, so unwillingly he had let her go.

She met Peter in the grounds on her way out.

'I am going to meet Alan at the 'Wheatsheaf', she said, her face pale and set, her manner more composed than it had been last night. 'In ten minutes' time I would like you to join us there, and Alan shall tell you the truth.'

Peter, bored with the whole affair, gave her a curt reply, promising to be there. He was certain of her guilt, and annoyed to think his cousin had ever met and fallen in love with her.

Paula walked on to the little tavern where Alan awaited her. His magnificent burgundy and silver car stood outside the little ivy-covered inn.

She felt cold and nervy when she finally faced him in a stuffy, dark little bar-parlour which smelt of stale beer. After a sleepless night she looked pale and worn. Yet she was beautiful — nothing could detract from Paula's magnificent colouring — and she looked slender and graceful in pale lavender. Alan looked at her in silent admiration for a few seconds.

'She's terrific,' he thought, pleased and soothed by the sight of her. 'Can't think why I ever let her escape me in Paris.'

Paula looked at him with a frozen expression in her eyes. She hated that slight, elegant form — that sleek, fair head. His handsome face meant nothing to her now. She knew the cruelty, the selfishness, the lack of feeling behind it.

'Now I am here, tell me why you want to see me,' she said curtly.

'My dear girl,' he said in the lazy, drawling voice which held a caressing note painfully familiar to her, 'don't look at me as though you could murder me.'

'I could — willingly,' broke from Paula. 'I loathe and despise you!'

'Oh, come,' he said, drawing nearer her. 'I'm not going to stand for that. Once you loved me — very much too. D'you think I've forgotten how you used to kiss me and want my kisses?'

She blushed scarlet.

'Yes — you remember that — and humiliate me by the memory,' she said, nodding, a note of indescribable bitterness in her voice. 'But it doesn't alter facts. I hate you now, Alan, as much as I once cared. You killed my love. You took me from my home, swearing to protect me, to marry me, and then you tried to — ' She broke off, burying her face in her hands. 'You were horrible!' she added in a stifled tone.

Alan's handsome face reddened slightly.

'Look here, Paula, I'm sorry about Paris,' he said. 'I admit I behaved badly.'

She raised her head.

'You admit it?'

'Yes. I'm sorry I didn't marry you, Paula.'

'It is too late to be sorry about that now. But if you see the wrong you did me, you can make reparation — make amends now.'

'Yes, I can, and will,' he said eyeing her strangely and folding his arms on his chest.

'You mean that? You will tell Peter Westbury that I was tricked into calling myself your wife that night?' She spoke eagerly, a slight quiver to her lower lip. 'Oh, Alan, if you will do that I will be grateful all my life.'

His dark blue eyes narrowed.

'You are so crazy about this fellow, Strange, that you would give anything to get rid of me and marry him in peace, eh?'

She thought he was being sympathetic and understanding, and meant to help her. An involuntary rush of gratitude, of relief, brought tears to her eyes.

'Yes, I love Jack Strange — with all my heart, Alan. And Jack loves me. There is nothing between us except the shadow of that night in Paris and Peter Westbury's suspicions. If you will tell him the truth he will keep quiet and leave me alone, and I shall be happy.'

Her innocent admission of genuine love and admiration for Jack secretly infuriated Alan. With every passing moment his desire to win her back was increasing — he would make her care again — make her forget Jack Strange — even if he had to relinquish his freedom for marriage.

'Listen, Paula,' he said. 'I have said I will make amends for what happened in Paris, and I will.'

'You will tell Mr. Westbury when he comes — ' Paula began eagerly.

'That I am willing to marry you — yes,' said Alan.

'That you are willing to marry me?' said Paula incredulously and slowly, as though Alan's words had stunned her.

'Yes,' said Alan, nodding.

She stared at him — tried hard to realise what he had said — what he meant. And suddenly her eyes widened, she drew a sharp breath.

'Willing — to — marry me!' she repeated breathlessly. 'Oh, what do you mean — how can you?'

'I mean what I say,' broke in Alan. He threw his cigarette end into the empty grate and came up to Paula, took her by both arms and looked hard into her eyes. 'I made a mistake in Paris,' he added. 'I admit I behaved badly — deceived you. Since you left me, I have come to the definite conclusion that I want you, Paula, and no other woman, for my wife. I repeat — I am willing to marry you, and as soon as you like, and I shall tell Westbury so.'

She shrank back from him, trembling in every limb. Her eyes gleamed with anger and fear.

'You must be mad,' she said. 'How dare you suggest marriage to me now — after all that has happened! I am engaged. Why, you know I am engaged — to Jack Strange. I love Jack — and I shall never marry any other man.'

Alan smiled disdainfully.

'Spare me your rhapsodies,' he drawled. 'They rather bore me, Paula, since I happen to be in love with you myself.'

'In love! You don't know the meaning of the word! You degrade it!' she said passionately. 'Let me go! Let go of my arms at once!'

His handsome eyes darkened.

'You aren't very affectionate these days, my dear,' he said. 'However, perhaps when we're married you'll cure that sharp temper you've so recently developed and be as charming as you used to be.'

'No,' she said, struggling violently to release herself. 'I can never feel anything but loathing and contempt for you. And I shall never marry you!'

He suddenly let her go. She stepped back, shaking now, indignant, her eyes flashing. He drew out a silver case and tapped a cigarette on it slowly, keeping his gaze fixed on her. His expression was inscrutable now. He was burning with the desire to crush her in his arms. Any show of indifference from a woman was calculated to make Alan Rivers more eager. He coveted the thing difficult or impossible to obtain. In the past, when Paula had clung to him, adored him, he had been mildly amused and attracted. But now he found her more than ever beautiful and desirable. He was not going to allow Jack Strange to marry her. He was not going to allow her to turn her back on him, scorn him like this. He was going to have her himself.

For the moment, though, he would curb his passionate longing to take her in his arms. Coolly he lit his cigarette.

'Now listen, Paula,' he said in a quiet voice. 'It's no use struggling and quarrelling like this. Let's discuss things sensibly.'

'I wish to discuss things sensibly,' she said, trying to speak with equal calm, though her heart was beating at a suffocating speed and her cheeks were pale. 'But if you try to touch me again, Alan, I shall walk out of the place.'

His tongue explored his cheek.

'We won't analyse your feelings towards me,' he said. 'We'll just take facts. I am willing to marry you, and I shall tell Peter Westbury so.'

'But I am not willing to marry you. Oh, can't you understand?' she cried. 'I love Jack Strange, and I am going to marry him.'

'Once you loved me. Does he know that?'

'No — he doesn't know.'

'You haven't dared to tell him?'

'I am innocent,' she said. 'But I haven't dared to tell him — you are right — because he could so easily misconstrue my presence in your flat that night.'

'Just as Westbury misconstrued it.'

'Yes.'

'It stands to reason that Jack would not marry you if he knew you had been in my flat in Paris — as Mrs. Rivers.'

'Probably not,' she said in a low voice. 'But even if he offered to marry me — he would have a doubt at the back of his mind unless you told him what actually happened, and — '

'Cleared the way for the happy day?' he said sarcastically.

'Yes.'

Alan laughed loudly. He was in a cruel, exasperating mood, and the girl, staring at him with despair on her face, realised that it would need all her courage, all her patience, to deal with him. No use losing her temper or becoming violent.

'Alan,' she said, pleading, 'won't you please go away and leave me alone — leave me to marry the man I love, in peace?'

'I have nothing more to say except that I love you and am quite willing to marry you myself.'

'If you loved me you'd go away — you wouldn't torture me like this.'

'Sorry,' he said, 'I want you. What I want I usually get.'

'I shall never marry you.'

'Very well. As you like,' he said, shrugging his shoulders. 'But when Westbury turns up I will tell him I am willing to marry you.'

She stared at him with frightened eyes. She began to understand the game he was playing, and the knowledge terrified her.

'But don't you see what that implies — what he will think?'

'Yes, I see.'

'He will draw the wrong conclusions,' said Paula, clasping and unclasping her hands. 'He will think you are just offering marriage because you — I — in Paris — of — !' She broke off with a sharp cry, and her face paled again. 'It isn't fair — you can't let him think such a thing!' she added in a choked voice.

Just for a moment as he looked at her, Alan Rivers softened — felt ashamed of the way in which he was treating this girl. But the soft feeling speedily passed. The remembrance of her youthful, enchanting sweetness in the past quickened his desire to take her for his own.

He put an arm around her and drew her close.

'I love you — I want you!' he muttered. 'I won't give you up — no, I won't go away. It's no use asking me to.'

Paula felt utterly crushed and defeated. She was helpless. She could not defend herself, could not extricate herself from the tangle without Alan's help. And that help was definitely refused.

Shuddering, she drew away from his arm.

'Oh, what am I to do?' she whispered.

'You can make your own arrangements, Paula,' he said. 'I will marry you when and where you wish. The sooner you leave Marlborough the better.'

She did not answer. Despairing, hopeless, she looked through the dusty window of the bar-parlour, out at the sun-dappled road. She saw a car draw up and Peter's trim, familiar figure step out of it.

'Mr. Westbury has arrived,' she said drearily.

Peter came into the room looking bored and uncomfortable. Closing the door behind him, he looked from Alan to the girl.

'Well,' he said curtly, 'have you two finished your conversation? If so, I'd like just to know the whole truth and be done with it. I'm rather tired of the whole business.'

Paula swallowed hard — looked at him with clouded eyes.

'Mr. Westbury, you won't believe me,' she said, 'but I am innocent and Alan refuses to tell you the truth.'

Peter tightened his jaw.

'Miss Broughton, I'm not a child to be stuffed with stories of that kind,' he said briskly. 'If you are innocent, Rivers will tell me so. I'm really anxious to end the business, which is most unpleasant. But it is my duty to the family, and particularly to my cousin, to ask Rivers — about Paris.'

He paused and looked questioningly at Alan. The latter was staring hard at Paula. When he spoke, it was in a low, deliberate voice.

'I'd rather not bring up details of the past,' he said. 'All I can say is — as I have just told Paula — that I am quite willing to marry her as soon as she wishes.'

Complete silence. Peter Westbury was too well-bred to show by any expression on his face what effect those words had upon him.

'I see,' he said. 'Well, that is quite conclusive, Rivers.'

A hurt look crossed Paula's pale face. She turned to Peter and said in a tone of the most passionate resentment:

'He has no right to let you think such things of me. I am innocent — I have every right to marry Jack!'

'I regret,' said Peter crisply, 'that I can no longer believe what you say, nor look upon you as fit to be the future Lady Strange. I must ask you to end your engagement with my cousin today.'

'No — no — ' she began wildly.

'You must,' broke in Peter. 'Otherwise I shall be under the painful necessity of having to acquaint my cousin with the story of your association with Rivers.'

'He wouldn't believe it. He loves me — trusts me — he will take my word — '

'Against mine? — when I was introduced to you in Paris — in that flat — and told you were Mrs. Rivers?' said Peter in the same icy tone.

'Oh, you will drive me mad between you!' cried Paula, covering her face with her hands.

'Take my advice and don't make a fuss about this,' added Peter. 'It will only end in humiliation for you. I am quite willing to say nothing to Jack about your past if you choose to break the engagement quietly. You can easily — er — suggest you have made a mistake and leave 'The Whyspers' at once.'

'Made a mistake!' repeated Paula in a bewildered voice. 'When I love him more than life itself!'

'You can choose,' said Peter, moving uncomfortably. 'Either break the engagement and go — leaving him with — er — pleasant memories — or I shall be obliged to tell him the painful truth.'

'No — not the truth!' said Paula, looking at Alan bitterly. 'Lies — evil lies!'

He did not speak — only avoided her gaze. Peter moved towards the door.

'I leave it in your hands,' he said. 'If you have not broken your engagement with my cousin by tonight — I shall see that it is broken myself.'

Paula made no answer. Her head bowed, she was shivering, dazed with misery and the utter helplessness of her position. The bitter, terrible price she was paying for that blind love she had given Alan in the past! It was almost too much for her to bear. Alan Rivers and Peter Westbury between them were crushing her — crushing the very life from her. What could she do? Either she must break her engagement and leave Jack to regret her, just thinking she no longer cared — or ugly, base lies would be crammed down his throat by the cousin who was so anxious to maintain the honour and pride of the family. He would be aghast at the thought that his Paula, whom he had thought pure and innocent, had lived in Paris with Alan Rivers.

She might tell him her version of the story and beg him to believe her, and out of his honest love for her he might give her the benefit of the doubt and marry her. But it would be against his parents' wishes — with ugly suspicions all round her — and there must always be a doubt in his own mind which Alan Rivers was too cowardly to remove.

She was caught between the devil and the deep.

Whichever way she chose it would break her heart and his — they must separate. It was unspeakable that these two, who might have been so divinely happy together, must go their separate ways — all because of her innocent trust in Alan — and his ruthless desire to have her now.

When she looked up again Peter had gone. Alan, with a rather humble look on his handsome, selfish face, approached her, put out his hand.

'Paula, don't look like that,' he mumbled. 'You loved me once: surely you could love me again? I'll give you a wonderful time when you're my wife — take you abroad — buy you everything you want. I'll make you forget that other figure and — '

'Don't go on,' broke in Paula, pushing his hand away. 'I shall never marry you. You are forcing me to leave Jack and his home, but when I leave, it will be alone — not with you.'

'I shall follow you.'

'You may follow, but you will never win me back. I don't even hate you now. I feel something deeper than hatred. I despise you.'

Alan reddened.

'Paula, I'll make you pay for those words. I'll never leave you alone!' he said.

She did not answer. Pale, tense, eyes misty, she turned and walked out of the room, leaving him there.

Paula realised only when she reached

home that she had not been to the village and bought her surprise present for Jack, which she had said she was going to do, as an excuse for going out alone. But somehow it did not seem to matter. Nothing mattered now. It was the end of everything, she thought wretchedly.

Peter had returned to 'The Whyspers', and he was the first person she met in the hall. He met her gaze with a look that made her flinch and pale. But she walked up to him bravely.

'I have decided what to do,' she said in a low voice. 'I will — speak to Jack tonight and break my — engagement — since I am being forced to do so. You will — give me until tonight, won't you?'

Peter did not know why, but somehow, the obvious misery in the girl's eyes worried him. He answered rather curtly.

'Yes, you may have until tonight. And please remember it is your own fault that this has happened.'

She did not reply to that. With a bitter smile she turned away from him. At that moment, Jack appeared. The sight of his handsome face made Paula feel suddenly dizzy and faint. How could she drive that happy look from his eyes — and everything between them?

'Why, hullo, darling!' he said. 'You back already? I thought you'd be much longer, so I've just arranged to play tennis at the Whites. They rang up and asked me if I'd make a fourth.'

'Yes, of course,' murmured Paula, trying to smile.

He saw that she was very pale and swaying a little on her feet. He rushed forward and caught her in his arms.

Paula pulled herself together with great effort. The faintness passed. But the feel of his arms around her, the sight of that open, frank face bending over her in such distress, nearly broke her heart when she remembered what she must say and do tonight. For an instant she let him hold her, leaned her head against his shoulder, her lips brushing the sleeve of his coat.

'I'm quite all right, Jack. Stupid of me. I just felt very odd for a moment. The heat is stifling this morning. I didn't go to the shops after all — turned back,' she said rather incoherently.

He smoothed the coppery hair back from her forehead. His dark eyes were inexpressibly tender.

'Darling — I can't have you getting heatstroke or anything like that,' he said. 'Look here, I'll ring the Major and tell him I'm not coming.'

'No — no — you must go, Jack — yes, please do, to please me,' she said. 'I'm perfectly all right now.'

'Are you certain?' he said anxiously.

'Quite.'

She smiled at him and stroked his smooth, boyish head. Reassured, he dropped a swift kiss on her hair and let her go.

'Okay, then, sweetheart. Go up and lie down till lunch, will you?'

'Yes, I will.'

Peter, who had been standing by watching this little scene, his face wooden, asked himself whether she was to be pitied, or whether she was just a consummate actress. At any rate, he felt sorry for Jack — darned sorry, he thought. The boy was crazy about the girl, and would be terribly upset when she broke the engagement. Wretched business altogether!

'Peter is going to drive me to the Whites in the Rover, then bring it back, because mother wants it,' Jack was saying. 'See you at lunch. Mind you're better, Paula, darling. I don't much like leaving you. Goodbye.'

Paula, climbing wearily to her room, wondered what he would say when she told him tonight that she would be leaving him, not for a few hours, but for ever.

She wondered how she could face it. She began to consider whether or not she would write him a note and leave the house without seeing him. Perhaps that would be less agonising for them both. But whatever she did it would hurt — hurt incredibly. She had imagined she had suffered in Paris when she discovered Alan's true character and left him. But that was a pin-prick compared to this scorching, aching pain in her heart — the pain of losing Jack — and for no real fault or folly of her own.

She locked herself in her bedroom and lay down on the bed, having first drawn her blinds to shut out the brilliant sunshine.

'Oh, Jack, Jack!' She sobbed his name again and again, pressing her anguished face hard against the pillow lest anybody outside should hear her crying.

When her tears were spent, she lay silent and breathless; her slender body shaking, her eyes swollen and red. She tried then in a kind of numb despair to think what she must do. First she must part from Jack — then begin life again. But it would not be life — it would be existence — a dreary, grey existence in which love could play no part.

She must lie to Jack — tell him she had 'made a mistake' — then watch that charming face of his change from amazement to grief — from grief to contempt. He must, of course, be contemptuous of a love that could last so short a duration. Or if he thought she still cared and was going for some mysterious, inexplicable reason he would be pained and angry — yes — whatever happened he would not understand and she could not explain.

Five minutes before luncheon she was still lying there on her bed, struggling for composure, wondering how to face what lay before her. She was roused by a violent banging on her door.

She started and sprang to her feet, pushed the damp, crushed hair back from her tear-stained face and walked to the door.

'Yes?' she said in a calm voice. 'Who is it?'

'It's Gerry,' said a hoarse, frightened young voice, totally unlike the matter-of-fact tones of the normal Gerry. 'Oh, Paula, come quickly!'

Paula's heart missed a beat.

'What on earth is the matter?'

'An accident — an awful accident!' cried Gerry, breathing quickly. 'Jack — '

Paula flung open the door, forgetting her disordered appearance, her inflamed eyes.

'Jack? An accident to Jack?' she said tensely. 'What — what has happened, Gerry?'

'Peter went to the Whites in the Rover — to fetch Jack from tennis,' said Gerry. 'You know Crayton Hill — that awful hill halfway from the Whites? Well, something went wrong and Peter lost control.'

'Yes, yes!' cried Paula as Gerry paused. 'Oh, what — what has happened?'

'They crashed into a lorry,' continued the younger girl, hiding her face with her hands. 'Poor Peter was killed instantaneously, and they're bringing Jack home now. They — they think he's dying — '

4

'Dying?' repeated Paula incredulously.

'Yes,' cried Gerry. 'That's what they — they think. Mother went with Mr. Oliver to bring him home.'

Paula clasped both hands over a heart that seemed to have stopped beating. Her face was ashen.

'Why wasn't I told before?' she asked in a low voice. 'I ought to have helped to fetch him home too.'

Gerry ceased weeping, wiped her eyes and looked through swollen, red-rimmed eyes at the other girl.

'Nobody knew where you were,' she said almost sullenly. 'Mother did ask. But what does it matter? What does anything matter if Jack dies?'

She spoke with the hopelessness of the very young. Anyhow she had no love for Paula Broughton in her heart and did not particularly care how she suffered. But those words: 'What does anything matter if Jack dies' — echoed and re-echoed in Paula's brain.

Was it possible that she was about to lose the one great love of her life? She shivered at the thought. It could not be true. Fate could not pursue her so relentlessly.

Without another word she ran downstairs to the hall, oblivious of her dishevelled appearance — her tumbled hair and tear-stained face.

She reached the front door, flung it open and was just in time to see the Stranges' car driving very slowly up to the house. The funeral pace agonised her. Involuntarily, Paula put a hand to her mouth. She realised that she must pull herself together. But never before had she felt or understood the frightfulness of loss through a sudden and violent death — the loss of somebody who means literally everything.

The car stopped at last before the house, and the chauffeur, shocked and harassed, opened the door. The first person to step out was Jack's mother.

Paula looked at her anxiously. The old lady's face was pale as ivory, though wonderfully calm. Even in the presence of death itself, Lady Strange never lost her nerve or courage, nor exhibited extreme emotion in public. She was shaken and terrified by the accident to her son and nephew. But she did not show it. And somehow something of her marvellous composure in that moment, helped to soothe Paula's torn and shattered nerves.

'Jack — what has happened — ?' was all she could say in a whisper to Lady Strange as she ran to her and gripped her hands.

'My poor Paula,' said Lady Strange in a remote voice. 'This is terrible for you — as well as for us.'

'Jack — ' repeated the girl, tremulously.

'He is alive,' said Jack's mother.

'Oh, thank God!' said Paula.

'But only just,' added Lady Strange. 'He is very badly hurt. It was a frightful smash. The car was completely wrecked. Poor Peter — ' She shuddered. 'He was dead, and terribly injured.'

Paula could not even begin to think about Peter or what his death might mean to her. She only looked with dumb agony at the figure Jack Strange, being carried now by the chauffeur and Dr. Oliver out of the car. The doctor had applied first-aid on the spot, and the dark head of the injured man was half hidden by white bandages. Paula felt physically ill as she looked at him — lying with closed eyes against Dr. Oliver's arm. Could this be the gay, animated figure she had seen an hour or two ago — this helpless, unconscious figure with the bandaged head and bloodless face?

She drew back as the doctor and chauffeur walked slowly and carefully through the door into the hall. She caught a fuller glimpse of Jack's face as he was carried by, the lips twisted with pain.

With the numb feeling of one who is hurt — too hurt to feel any more pain — she followed Lady Strange up the stairs — followed Jack's unconscious figure.

It was just as though he was already dead. Why was there this presentiment in the house that he would die?

Sir James Strange, with Gerry hanging on to his arm, was at the top of the landing, also watching Jack being carried to his room. The old man's face was pathetic. It was his only son who was being brought home unconscious, dying — he was suffering the most cruel anxiety.

Jack was carefully laid on his bed. The chauffeur tiptoed out of the room, and Dr. Oliver bent over the insensible form. Sir James' valet was sent for to help him undress the helpless man. Paula found herself staring at a closed door. She felt horribly shut out. She wanted intensely to rush into that room, kneel beside Jack's bed, unobtrusively yet watchful. He would need her.

She knew he would need her as soon as he opened his eyes. His feelings were hers. They were always in mutual sympathy — always understood each other.

'Jack — ' she said aloud, in a queer, frightened little voice.

She felt Lady Strange's hand on her shoulder.

'Come, my dear — we musn't stay here now. Dr. Oliver and Martin will see to Jack, and Gerry is telephoning a nursing home which we know of in Marlborough. A trained nurse will soon be here.'

Paula turned and went with the old lady. The look of suffering on her face touched Jack's mother. She patted Paula's head.

'There, my child, don't look like that.'

Paula pressed her hand convulsively.

'I love him so — I can't bear it — '

'We both love him,' said Lady Strange in her gentle voice. 'And we must both be brave, Paula.'

137

Sir James had gone to his study and Lady Strange followed him there — her first duty was to comfort her husband. So Paula was left alone. She paced up and down the drawing-room, which was directly under Jack's bedroom, and with both hands pressed to her aching, throbbing heart, waited for Dr. Oliver to come down and tell her what he thought of Jack's chances.

Every footstep, every sound she heard above, increased her agony of fear — fear lest Jack should die. Was this to be an added punishment for her folly in Paris — an additional price to pay?

Luncheon was served, but nobody paid any attention to the meal. Nobody wanted to eat, so the meal was cleared away again.

An hour after Jack had been brought home, Paula was still alone in the drawing-room, walking up and down, up and down, her cheeks colourless.

Through the open window she saw Gerry, and with her Diana Cotesmore. Gerry had gone for her friend. The two were sitting on the lawn under the big cedar, Diana's arm was around Gerry. They were obviously consoling each other.

With hot, strained eyes, Paula stared at them. Why should Diana be here? Why should Gerry have sent for her? She, Jack's future wife, was an outsider here; unwanted, accepted only for Jack's sake. Never had she felt the position more cruelly than at this moment.

Then at last the drawing-room door opened, and Lady Strange came in. Her ivory face was calm as usual, although her eyes were rimmed with red. Paula fancied she spoke more coldly than usual and without any of the tenderness or pity she had shown a few moments ago.

'Jack is conscious,' she said. 'He has asked for you, and Dr. Oliver thinks you had better go to him just for a second, Paula.'

Paula's heart leaped wildly. He was awake — he had asked for her.

'No excitement, Paula,' added Lady

Strange. 'Be very quiet.'

Paula blushed vividly.

'I won't upset him, Lady Strange,' she said.

She felt that she comprehended the elder woman's attitude. She was jealous, of course — jealous because Jack's first request had been for his future wife. She was like most adoring mothers — innately jealous of the woman who takes first place in their son's hearts.

Paula smiled a little reflectively as she sped up to her Jack's room. Was everybody, even Jack's mother, to turn against her now that Jack was so helpless, so ill?

Dr. Oliver met her outside the door.

'Just a second — and don't excite him, Miss — er — Broughton,' he whispered.

'He isn't mine any more,' thought Paula. 'He is his mother's — he is Dr. Oliver's — he is anybody's but mine — I am only permitted to look at him —'

Aloud she said:

'What are his injuries, doctor?'

'Slight — very slight concussion. A broken left arm and severe cuts and bruises all over. It is shock from which he is suffering most acutely at the moment.'

'But will he recover?'

'Oh, yes — with time and care. But he must be very, very carefully nursed and treated. Any worry or fresh shock might kill him.'

'He will have every care here,' said Paula, clasping her hands. 'Oh, how thankful I am — I thought he was dying.'

'He has escaped death by a wonderful chance,' said the doctor gravely.

A moment later Paula was in the room, which was dim and full of the odour of antiseptics. The curtains were drawn, shutting out the bright sunlight. And in bed, his face drawn and white, his eyes closed, lay Jack, who loved the sunshine.

It wrenched the heart of the girl who

loved him to see him so reduced. She knelt beside him calmly, took one of his hands and pressed it gently between her own.

'Jack — ' she whispered.

His eyes opened. To Paula they looked dark with pain.

'Paula,' he murmured.

'I am here, my darling.'

'Darling, darling Paula — don't leave me.'

'No — no — never. I shall never leave you while you need me.'

'I'm sorry to have been — such a fool,' he said with difficulty. 'I shouldn't have let — Peter drive — my car. How is he?'

She dared not tell him that Peter Westbury was dead.

'All right — all right, darling. Don't worry about him — only get well and strong yourself, very soon.'

'Of course — I must — we are going to be married next month,' he said slowly, trying to smile at her.

She swallowed hard, trying to be

142

brave and composed. Leaning down she kissed him on the lips.

'Of course, Jack — ' she murmured.

'Don't — leave me,' he said again. 'I love you so, Paula — ' Then his eyes closed, and he drifted into unconsciousness again.

Paula got up and looked up at the doctor. Her beautiful eyes were bright with unshed tears.

'He wants me,' she said. 'Ought I — to go?'

'He will sleep now for a bit,' said Dr. Oliver. 'The nurse will be here shortly. When she comes, I'll give an order that you are to be sent for whenever he wants you. It won't do to upset him in anything just now — his temperature will go up at once if he gets excited or distressed.'

He told Jack's mother the same thing. It very soon became apparent to them all at 'The Whyspers' that Paula was the most necessary person in the world to Jack — that she must be allowed to see him before anybody else.

But it did not gain favour for Paula. It had the opposite effect. The family were jealous and resentful of Jack's love for her. They withdrew themselves into a cold reserve. Paula was left outside, alone, to suffer her anxiety on Jack's behalf. It hurt her, wounded her gentle, sensitive nature beyond measure. Yet she was proud and happy that Jack loved and needed her. She was ready to do absolutely anything for him.

* * *

That evening there was no change in Jack's condition. He was still seriously ill. He slept at intervals, drugged. When he was not sleeping he was in pain, and had one incessant call — for Paula.

She sat beside him quietly, holding his hand, soothing him. The doctor and the hospital nurse now in attendance thought they had never seen anything more touching than the look on her face as she bent over him.

But downstairs there were bitter

feelings against her.

'She seems to have bewitched him,' Gerry said in her blunt, outspoken way. 'He hasn't asked to see anybody, even mother — '

Lady Strange, her gentle face unusually hard, bit her lip.

'Jack is very devoted to his future wife,' she said with an effort.

But Gerry knew that she was jealous — bitterly envious of the girl who was sitting upstairs with the injured man.

Diana Cotesmore, still in the house, said nothing, but thought much. In her queer, selfish fashion, she, too, was suffering. She was madly in love with Jack Strange — more than ordinarily jealous of Paula. It enraged her to know that at this very moment Paula was upstairs, at Jack's side.

She was spitefully pleased when, after dinner that same night, Alan Rivers called at the house and asked for Paula. It put Paula in a bad light to have this young man constantly pursuing her. Lady Strange received him coldly; then, remembering he had been at school with Peter Westbury, softened a trifle.

'It must have been a shock to you to know that poor Peter was killed in the accident,' she said.

Alan, spruce, handsome, over-polite, as usual, inclined his head.

'I was very shocked,' he admitted. 'I heard about it at my hotel. I can't believe Peter is dead.'

'He was killed outright — mercifully,' sighed Lady Strange.

'And Jack?'

'In a critical condition, but we have every hope that he will recover.'

'I came to offer my sympathies to Paula,' said Alan smoothly. 'But if it is not convenient just now — '

'Not at all,' said Jack's mother. 'I will send for her. She is sitting with my son at the moment, but I may, perhaps, take her place while she talks to you — '

Across the room Diana Cotesmore's blue eyes met Alan's. A queer little smile hovered about her mouth. Alan flickered his eyebrows slightly. These

146

two seemed suddenly to understand each other. Diana was practically certain in that moment that Alan was in love with Paula — and trying to take her from Jack. The thought both enraptured and excited her.

It came as a shock to Paula when Gerry crept into her brother's room and whispered in her ear that Alan wanted to see her.

She left Jack with the greatest reluctance. As she followed Gerry downstairs her cheeks burned and her lips tightened at the thought of Alan. How dared he follow her here like this — worry her — when Jack's life was in danger.

His coming brought back to her mind all the happenings of the last twenty-four hours. Her heart gave a twist of dismay as she suddenly recollected her last meeting with Alan. She had been forced by Peter to promise to break her engagement with Jack.

But must she do it now that Peter

was dead? She bore him no grudge. She knew he had acted according to his own code — yet she felt his death to be a release for her — a release from her promise to break that engagement which meant so much to her. Only Alan remained to threaten and torture her. But would he prove as ruthless, as relentless as Peter had been — now that this terrible accident had taken place?

Hope sprang to Paula's heart. Almost eagerly she approached Alan. She must see him, speak to him alone, implore him to put an end to her misery and go away tomorrow. Surely now that Peter was no more he would leave her alone? It was Peter who had been the more imminent danger — who had seen her that fatal night in Alan's flat.

She tried to greet Alan carelessly.

'It is nice of you to come and sympathise,' she forced, giving him her hand. 'But I — I'm afraid I can't stay just now. I — Jack wants me upstairs — '

'I daresay Jack won't mind if I take

your place for a moment,' put in Lady Strange with a slightly acid smile.

Paula reddened. She felt rather than saw the sneer on Diana's beautiful face — heard Gerry's subdued snigger. She knew they were all jealous — against her. But she spoke very gently to Jack's mother.

'Why, of course — please do go to him — he is awake at the moment.'

Alan's deep blue eyes narrowed a trifle. In his quick, astute way he summed up the whole situation and was fully aware of the strained atmosphere in this household. Paula was by no means wanted here. But he wanted her — how he wanted her — ! He looked down at her beautiful face, her lovely bronze head, and felt an insane desire to seize her in his arms.

'Perhaps you'd just walk down the main drive with me to the gate, Paula,' he said. 'I'll come again tomorrow when you are less occupied.'

'Do,' she forced. 'Yes, of course, I'll walk with you.'

'Jack ought to know how she flirts like mad with this fellow,' Gerry whispered to Diana.

Diana made no answer. But she smiled.

In the garden Alan and Paula walked down the drive.

'Why did you come?' Paula broke the silence between them. 'You must have known I would not want to see you tonight. Jack is desperately ill.'

'Of course, I'm very sorry about the accident. It is a hellish business,' said Alan glibly. 'And it's awful to think of poor Peter — '

Paula shivered.

'Awful,' she repeated. 'And Jack might have died, too — '

Alan paused and took one of her slender wrists in a steel-like grasp.

'Stop a moment, Paula. I want to talk to you,' he said. 'You appear to have forgotten the way our conversation ended this morning.'

She stiffened. Her face, upturned to

his, was like a pale mask in the moonlight.

'No — I haven't forgotten. I couldn't possibly forget the filthy way you lied to Peter — the way in which you allowed him to think things of me.'

Alan tongue in cheek, asked:

'Are you going to waste time reproaching me, Paula?'

'No,' she said breathlessly, her heart racing. 'But I am going to ask you to be decent, to be generous, in view of Peter's terrible death and of Jack's accident, to go away and end this forever.'

His handsome face assumed its obstinate look.

'I won't go away unless you come with me.'

'Oh, am I to argue, to plead with you all over again?' she cried under her breath.

'Don't waste your time,' he said. 'I love you — I mean to have you, Paula.'

'You can't make me break my engagement.'

'I can, and will. Unless you break it, I shall tell the Stranges, myself, that you lived with me in Paris as my wife.'

'That's a lie!'

Her voice was passionate and resentful, but he laughed and caught her other wrist.

'Is it? Well, let's make it true. Come with me to Paris — run away with me all over again, Paula, and this time I swear I'll make you my wife.'

With loathing in her eyes, she tried to drag her hands away.

'I hate you — despise you! Let me go!'

It amused him, soothed his wounded vanity, his thwarted passion, to use sheer physical force on her tonight. He let her writhe and struggle in vain, then flung both arms around her.

'No use — you can't get away from me, Paula,' he said in a low, tense voice.

He pressed his lips hard on her mouth. It was a long, ruthless kiss that revolted and terrified her. When at last he released her, she was pale and stricken. Loving Jack with all her heart and soul, it was like death itself to her to be in the arms of this other man.

She covered her face with her hands and began to sob in a broken, frightened way.

'Why, why must you torture me? Why can't you go away and leave me alone?'

'Because I want you to myself.'

She raised a face that streamed with tears.

'Have you no pity, no real decency in you, Alan? I love Jack Strange.'

'You loved me first. You can love me again.'

'Listen,' she said, trying to stifle her sobs. 'The doctor told me this morning that to distress or excite Jack in any way might kill him. If I were to leave him, disillusion him now, it might cause his death. Do you want that on your conscience?'

Alan averted his gaze.

'No, I don't.'

'Then at least leave me alone until he is better. I ask it for his sake only.'

Alan shrugged his shoulders.

'Oh, very well. I'll leave you in peace until Strange is better. But I'll remain in Marlborough. I'm not going to lose sight of you, Paula. And as soon as Strange is well, you must break that engagement — or I will do it for you!'

She dabbed at her eyes and strangled a heart-broken sigh. She was terribly tired — tired of fighting this man — of fighting for the happiness of the man she loved, as well as for her own.

'Very well,' she said. 'Now go, please!'

'Goodnight, Paula.'

He raised his hat, then turned and walked quickly down the drive where he was lost to view in the darkness.

Paula wiped her eyes, smoothed her hair, then started to walk back to the house. She had only one desire — to get back to Jack, to comfort him, help him over his moments of pain, soothe the poor nerves that had been torn to shreds.

But half-way down the garden she paused with a violent start. The tall figure of Diana Cotesmore appeared very suddenly from behind some bushes. Paula looked at her with wide, frightened eyes.

'Oh, how you startled me!' she murmured, trying to laugh.

Diana's face was curiously excited. She came up to Paula and stood looking at her in silence for an instant. Then she said, in a cool, modulated voice.

'I won't mince matters; I may as well tell you at once that I was on my way home just now, coming down a side path instead of the main drive, and I overheard your whole conversation with Alan Rivers.'

Paula's heart seemed to stop beating.

'You — heard — ?'

'Yes. I know now exactly what you are. And I wonder what my friends the Stranges would say,' said Diana in a slow, insulting voice, 'if they knew their son was engaged to be married to Alan's mistress?'

Paula's face went ashen, her body

shook from head to foot, as she gasped out a trembling, burning denial of the guilt attributed to her.

'It isn't true — it isn't true! Oh, how dare you say such a thing! I am not — I never have been his — his — oh! — ' She broke off and buried her face in her hands.

But Diana felt neither pity nor doubt about it. She put one hand on her hip and gave Paula a cruel, hard look.

'I'm sorry, Paula,' she said in a cool, drawling voice, 'but I cannot possibly believe anything you say. I overheard the entire conversation between you and Alan. It was conclusive evidence of what you are — what you have been.'

Paula uncovered her face. Her head shot up.

'It isn't true!' she repeated passionately. 'I am not what you think — what the conversation led you to believe. I will tell you the whole story, if you will only listen.'

'No, thank you,' said Diana coldly.

'I'd prefer not to hear your sordid story.'

'It isn't fair,' said the younger girl, her beautiful eyes flashing, her slight body drawn to its full height. 'You must listen to me!'

'Must I?' she said. 'I'd really rather not. However, if you insist — carry on. It won't alter my belief — my conviction of what you are. And from what I can gather, poor Peter knew what you were, too.'

'He made the same mistake you are making,' said Paula, putting her hands to her cheeks, which were scarlet, feverishly burning with embarrassment now. 'Since you listened to my conversation with Alan, didn't you hear me accuse him of lying to Peter?'

'Oh, I heard — yes,' drawled Diana. 'But that won't cut any ice. Alan made violent love to you — begged you to run away with him to Paris again — said he'd marry you this time — suggested he could break your engagement for you if you wouldn't

157

break it yourself.'

'Oh, yes, it all sounds awful — as though I'm guilty,' said Paula. 'But I can explain, Diana — I swear I can. Please, please be sensible and listen — without prejudice.'

Diana twisted her mouth — shrugged her shoulders again.

'Go on — tell me, then,' she said.

Paula prayed for courage, for strength. She was so tired, so worn with fighting — so sick about the whole affair. She had been through these very same arguments and accusations with Peter. Now he was dead — and she was facing the battle with a fresh enemy — with Diana Cotesmore. And she realised that Diana was an even more deadly opponent than Peter had been, because she was a woman — and a woman who wanted Jack Strange for herself.

Desperately she blurted out the whole story of her elopement with Alan — his deceit — her escape from the Paris flat.

'I swear by all I hold sacred that I

have told you the truth,' she finished in an impassioned voice. 'And that I love Jack with all my heart and soul — have only Jack's happiness at heart.'

As her voice died away, Diana stared a moment up at the starry sky, thinking, putting two and two together. She was a clever girl — a shrewd one. She knew that Paula had spoken the truth. She believed that story — was certain Paula was an innocent victim. Alan was a bad lot. It was all pretty obvious to Diana. But she had not the smallest intention of letting Paula know she believed her.

If Jack lived — and she believed he would, she wanted him for herself — wanted him crazily. If she could shake his faith in Paula — separate them finally — she might stand an excellent chance of catching Jack on the rebound.

'Well?' came Paula's voice, in an anguish of anxiety. 'Don't you believe me?'

Very slowly, deliberately, came Diana's answer.

'No.'

Paula uttered a cry.

'But you must — you must! Diana, I swear — '

'Please don't prolong this painful scene,' broke in Diana. 'I do not believe you. I am certain you are not what Jack believes you to be. I won't argue or discuss the matter further.'

Paula's heartbeats seemed to suffocate her. Her curly head bowed. She put a hand to her forehead with a gesture of infinite weariness and agony. She had suffered much, fought so desperately, she felt she could not suffer or fight very much longer. Everybody appeared to be out to separate her from Jack. It was useless trying to establish an innocence she could not prove — that Alan refused to admit.

'What do you mean to do?' she asked in a dull voice.

'Tell Lady Strange at once,' said Diana.

'If you do that — if you let Jack know — it might kill him,' said Paula, closing her eyes. 'He is very, very ill. Perhaps you forget that. Even Alan' — her voice broke on a bitter laugh — 'even Alan is going to wait until Jack is better, before he forces me to break my engagement.'

Diana bit her lower lip. What Paula said was true. Jack asked incessantly for his fiancée. It might prove fatal to cause an upheaval while he was still in that state of shock and collapse.

'I don't intend to let Jack suffer — at the moment,' she said, after a pause. 'I quite realise that you have wormed your way round him very cleverly, and that he wants you at this crisis. But as soon as the doctors say he is strong enough to bear it, I shall ask you to break your engagement.'

'Diana, you are a friend of Jack's — but not one of the family, as Peter was — do you honestly think you have any right to interfere — to insult me?'

'Every right,' said Diana, tossing her golden head. 'Before you came, I expected to become Jack's future wife — but you took him away from me.

Once you have gone back to where you belong, I shall probably take your place. Do you see?'

Those words were literally flung at Paula — calculated to hurt, to crush what spirit remained in her. They had the desired effect. Paula turned away, her face masked in pain. Perhaps Diana spoke the truth, she thought. Perhaps in days to come Jack would forget her — and take Diana for his wife.

'Oh, why should I have to bear so much when I am absolutely innocent of wrong!' she cried, half aloud. 'Oh, Jack, my darling, how can I leave you — '

'I will undertake to keep quiet about you until Jack is well,' came Diana's cold, hard voice. 'And when that time comes, I hope you will spare me the unpleasant necessity of informing him what you are, by breaking your engagement and going right away.'

Paula turned round and gave her a long, deep look — an odd look that made Diana feel strangely uncomfortable.

'Yes, I will do that,' she said in a hollow voice. 'You and Alan between you leave me no choice. But I hope for your sake, Diana, that you will never suffer as you are making me suffer. Good-night.'

Diana did not answer. She frowned and turned away from Paula, and walked quickly down the drive to the gates. She could do nothing more tonight. She was going home. But she hated Paula with unreasoning hatred — was aflame with jealousy because she knew Paula would now be returning to Jack's bedside.

'Not for long, though,' she told herself with almost fiendish pleasure. 'Once he is strong enough, Miss Paula will be turned out of 'The Whyspers'. Her day will be over, and mine will begin!'

The nurse in charge of Jack's case told Lady Strange that Paula was undoubtedly responsible for Jack's speedy recovery. The comfort of her presence, the knowledge of her love for him, on that first day, had given him the strength to fight a fierce battle with his shattered central nervous system and a high temperature.

After that it was a question of rest, quiet, and time for the broken arm to heal. Within a week of the accident he was on the road to recovery. Dr. Oliver said that he had a magnificent constitution and that later in his convalescent days it would be only weakness that he would have to conquer.

They were forced to tell him within a few days of the accident that his cousin had been killed instantaneously. He took the news well, although it upset him badly.

'Poor Peter — poor chap,' he said to Paula, his boyish face pale and gloomy. 'What a frightful thing! I wish I'd driven the car myself. Peter didn't understand it so well as I did. But the brakes might have gone wrong with me. I suppose it was fate — and couldn't be avoided. Poor Peter!'

At the end of a week he was much

better, and the arm was beginning to heal, carefully set and in a splint. Then began the worst time for Paula.

Alan had kept away from her during the last few days, but he was still there — an ever-present menace to her peace of mind. And Diana Cotesmore was an even more imminent danger. She was a near neighbour and constant visitor to 'The Whyspers', and she had just that little and dangerous knowledge of Paula's past. Paula knew she was waiting — waiting for the hour when she would be forced to end her engagement.

It was a ghastly position. Diana kept her promise to say nothing to the family for the moment. But she treated Paula frigidly in public, and with insulting contempt if ever she saw her alone. The family were not altogether charming to Paula. Lady Strange harboured a slight resentment against her because Jack had constantly asked for her in his illness, and Geraldine Strange had never liked or welcomed her as a future relative. Sir James was the only person in the house to treat Paula with kindness, and that was because he bore her no resentment, and was not jealous of her. But even he wished secretly that his son had chosen a girl like Diana Cotesmore.

It took all Paula's courage to stand up against things those days. But for Jack's sake she shouldered her burden and never once complained of her treatment — never allowed him to be depressed or anxious about their future happiness.

It was Jack's wish that they should get married as soon as he was well enough. And Paula let him make plans — let him talk of their future — agonised by the secret knowledge that those plans could never be carried out — those hopes never materialise. She knew her love and tenderness helped to make him well and strong and that he was making big strides towards recovery because he was so anxious to arrange their marriage.

But her heart was breaking — aching with the thought that soon — terribly soon now — she would be going away — making some futile excuse to break their engagement.

Diana was waiting to oust her. Alan was waiting to follow and persecute her.

There came the day when Diana met her alone in the lounge coming in from the garden, and stopped her.

'Paula — Jack is much better,' she said coldly. 'Lady Strange tells me he may be allowed to come down tomorrow.'

'Quite right,' said Paula, unhappily. 'But he is only up in a chair for the first time, and very weak. You can't mean — '

'I mean that you must start making your arrangements to break with him and leave here,' said Diana.

'He is very weak yet — ' Paula's voice tremulously.

'I know that,' said Diana remorselessly. 'But in, say, another five days Jack will be able to bear the — er

— unfortunate news. You wish to go quietly and without fuss. Well — make your plans to do so. That is all I have to say.'

She moved away, leaving Paula standing there alone, her heart jerking painfully, her mind full of unhappy, anguished thoughts.

Jack had got up today for the first time. Now, after lunch, he was resting, and Paula had been out for some fresh air and exercise. She was just going back to him. He hated letting her out of his sight. It was a quarter to four and she knew he would be awake — would want to sit up in his chair again and talk to her.

She was about to move up the wide oak staircase, when a shadow blotted out the bright sunlight from the open fronty door. She looked up and saw Alan standing there. He had walked quietly up the drive. She had not even heard him come. She looked at him dully, without resentment or anger — with nothing but despair in her beautiful eyes.

'May I come in, Paula?' he greeted her.

'What do you want?' she said quietly.

'You, of course,' he said boldly, advancing to her side. He lifted one of her hands and raised it to his lips. She recoiled, drawing the hand away, and shivered.

'Please don't!' she protested.

Alan raised his brows, eyed her a second in silence. He was almost shocked at her appearance. He had not seen her since the night of Jack's accident. She had grown very much thinner and paler. The strain of Jack's illness, coupled with the knowledge that she was being driven to leave him, had been eating Paula's very heart — straining all her nerves. She looked utterly worn.

'Are you all right? You don't look very well,' Alan said rather awkwardly.

She laughed mirthlessly.

'I'm not — bursting with health and happiness,' she said. 'Every day I've felt that I'm drawing near — a kind of death!'

Alan's weak face reddened.

'Do you care for the fellow as much as that, Paula?'

'Yes, as much as that.'

'It isn't very complimentary to me that you should have forgotten me so quickly,' he said.

'Please don't let us start a discussion,' she said wearily. 'Why have you come?'

'To say it's about time you came away with me,' he said sullenly, staring at her.

'I'm not coming with you. When I go it will be alone. But Jack is still weak and I — I haven't told him yet — ' Her voice faltered.

Alan suddenly gripped both hands and drew her toward him.

'You must tell him soon, then,' he said savagely. 'I'm sick of waiting for you. And you are coming with me — you belong to me — you loved me before you loved him — '

Paula was about to answer, to draw away her hands. But another voice interrupted Alan, a familiar voice, which sent the blood rushing to her cheeks, and made her heart miss a beat. She swung round and looked up at the first landing. To her horror she saw Jack, leaning over the banisters, staring down at her and Alan. He was in a blue dressing-gown, his arm still in its splint and sling. He had apparently walked out of his bedroom while the nurse was off-duty, heard voices downstairs, and had leaned over and seen Paula and Alan. His eyes looked stricken. His voice was hoarse as he called down to the girl.

'Paula! — tell me it isn't true — tell me that you don't belong to him — that you aren't going away with him!'

Paula tore her hands away from Alan's and rushed to the top of the stairs. Trembling, aghast, she stared up at Jack, much too agitated to think, for a moment, what to say to him. Her main feeling in that instant was fear for him, not for herself. She knew that he was still weak and ill; that a shock like this might undo all the good that had been done.

Jack started to stumble down the stairs, clinging to the banisters with the uninjured hand.

'Paula — Paula!' he stammered. 'What does this man mean — how can you belong to him? How can you go away with him, when you love me, are going to marry me? Paula — '

She gave a stifled cry, then ran forward up the stairs, two at a time, and met Jack in the bend of the staircase.

'Darling, don't come down — you aren't nearly strong enough,' she said. 'Go back — come with me — back to your room, darling.'

He swayed a moment where he stood. She could see that he was shaking from head to foot. He stared down at her with those stricken eyes of his — eyes filled with such agony, such dazed incredulity, such fear, it nearly broke her heart.

'No, I must speak to Rivers — he said you belonged to him. Oh, Paula, say it isn't true!'

'Hush, come back to your room — I — Jack, you aren't strong enough to argue with Alan,' Paula began desperately.

Her one clear thought was for him — anxiety lest this should prove too much for him in his weak condition. She put an arm about his waist.

'Come back to your room, darling,' she urged. 'I — I'll explain up there.'

'No — here, now — with Alan present,' said Jack thickly. His eyes seemed to burn into hers. 'Let me go — let me get down to him, Paula. Either he has done me an injury or he has insulted you — I want to know.'

'Jack,' she said, her heart pounding with fear for him. He looked livid, terrifying. 'Oh, please, please leave it now, come back with me to your room.'

For the first time in his life Jack Strange looked at her with doubt, mistrust in his gaze. She flinched as she read what was written in his eyes. But she still fought desperately to save him.

'Come, darling,' she urged. 'Come with me.'

Jack gazed past her, down to the tall, fair man who stood in the hall fingering his lips, looking very awkward and extremely annoyed. A sudden fury of resentment against Alan surged within him. How dare he say that Paula belonged to him — that she had ever loved him!

He staggered down two steps, past Paula, blood rushing to his temples.

'Liar!' he said thickly. 'Liar!'

Only those two words, those two steps. Then the world spun around him. He put out his uninjured hand — grappling with the darkness that came over him.

'Paula!' he called out.

She reached him as he lost consciousness, and had just sufficient strength to support him in her arms and let him fall gently on to the stairs, so that the broken arm did not suffer.

He lay there crumpled up, silent, eyes closed. She bent over him.

'Jack, Jack — '

She knew that the fool's paradise in which they had lived was finished. Jack would never believe in her or want her again. Her real punishment was beginning in this hour — an undeserved judgment for a sin she had never committed. But who would believe her?

Alan came quickly up the stairs. When he had seen Jack stagger and fall he had wished, for a fleeting moment, that he had let them alone. He touched the kneeling girl on the shoulder.

'Paula,' he said in a low voice, 'I'm sorry — '

'Oh, go — go away!' she cried with passionate emphasis. 'You've done enough harm.'

'Paula, you'd far better come away with me — ' he began.

She had no time to answer. At that moment, Geraldine Strange and Diana Cotesmore appeared in the lounge. They were strolling together from the drawing-room, laughing and talking. Then as they simultaneously caught sight of the huddled group on the bend of the staircase, they both stood still and stared.

Gerry caught sight of her brother's dark head cradled on Paula's arm. She gave a cry and rushed towards him.

'Jack! It's Jack!'

'Jack!' echoed Diana. She followed Gerry, her face hot with excitement and consternation.

'What's happened? What's happened?' Gerry gasped in an hysterical voice. 'Oh, look at him — he looks as though he were dead — '

Paula looked up at Jack's young sister, appealingly.

'No, no, Gerry — he isn't dead — he has fainted — he insisted on coming down the stairs,' she stammered. 'Send for the nurse — we must get him up to his room.'

Gerry swung round on Alan, looked at him with suspicion and resentment.

'What are you doing here?' she asked rudely.

He flushed and began to walk down the stairs. As he passed Diana, she gave him a look full of inquiry. He met it — shrugged his shoulders.

'I'm sorry,' he murmured. 'Mr. Strange overheard a conversation between Paula and myself — er — he didn't like it. I'd better go, I suppose.'

'Ah!' said Diana under her breath.

Exultation gripped her. She could guess exactly what had happened. Jack had accidentally come upon a revealing scene between Alan and Paula. Oh, well, it was bound to happen sooner or later! Why not now? It was high time Paula left this house for ever.

Without a trace of pity she walked to Paula's side.

'Leave Jack alone,' she said in a tone of command. 'His nurse — his sister — or I — will see to him.'

Paula's head shot up.

'How dare you — ' she began.

'It's no good trying to brazen it out,'

interrupted Diana cruelly. 'I can see what has happened. Jack has found out at last what you are. You had better pack up your things and follow Alan.'

Gerry stared at her friend.

'Di — what are you saying?' she gasped.

'You'll know soon,' said Diana. 'I'll explain to you all later. We'd better get Jack back to bed, now.'

Paula grew quite calm — with the despairing calm of one who knows it is no use fighting any longer — that the odds were against her and it was best to surrender quietly.

Diana knew — Diana would tell the family now. And Jack knew too. Not much — but enough to shake his faith in her and perhaps destroy his love. With aching eyes she looked down at his drawn face. He was still blessedly unconscious — and at peace. But once he recovered consciousness he would suffer horribly. And she could do nothing to prevent it — to lessen his pain.

In a sort of stupor she rose from her knees. Gerry, only too pleased to see her humiliated and hurt, had thrust her roughly away and was supporting her brother's head on her arm now.

The hospital nurse, flustered and agitated, came hurrying down the stairs to her patient.

Paula was pushed to one side. Diana, Gerry, and the nurse, between them, lifted the unconscious man and carried him up to his room. Sir James and Lady Strange were in the garden, happily ignorant of the drama taking place in the house.

Paula found herself quite alone — she had been shut out — for good. She knew exactly what would happen. If she tried to see Jack she would be insulted and turned away.

Quite probably, when he first came to his senses, he would ask for her — demand to see her — to hear her explanation of everything. She asked herself, dully, what to do — to stay and explain and beg him to believe in her innocence — or to go away without seeing him again.

Supposing she told him what had happened and implored him to believe in her — supposing he said he would believe, despite all that Alan had to say or suggest — supposing, out of his great love for her, he begged her to remain here and marry him, just the same? Could she stay and become his wife, knowing there must be some doubt in the back of his mind — that at times he might be suspicious and distrustful? And all his people would be against the marriage — hate her, look upon her as an interloper.

Paula covered her eyes with her hands. She was tortured beyond endurance by her thoughts — her imagination. And she knew, when she had thought everything over and considered every possibility, that she could not stay and marry Jack, even if he wanted her to do so. She could never bear the moments of doubt and disbelief. And Alan was quite merciless; would never clear her.

There was only one thing left for her to do — to go away without seeing Jack again.

She let her arms drop to her sides limply. Like a shadow she moved slowly up the stairs to her own room.

Diana Cotesmore met her, a quarter of an hour later, coming out of that room, dressed for travelling and carrying a suitcase. She was colourless, but quite composed. Diana openly scrutinised her, arrogant and in command.

'So you are going!' she said. 'Very wise.'

'Yes, I am going,' said Paula quietly. 'If you will be kind enough to ask the chauffeur to drive me to the station I'll pick up a train for town when I can.'

'Very well,' said Diana in a frigid voice.

'I am going because I think it best — for Jack,' added Paula, looking down at the ground, 'not because I am guilty.'

There was something so quiet, so simple, so brave about her in this moment that even Diana felt a tinge of shame as she looked at her.

'I don't know what to think,' she muttered, 'but I'm sure it's best for you to go.'

'Yes,' said Paula in a strangled voice. 'Is Jack — better?'

'He is beginning to come round,' said Diana in a grudging voice. 'The nurse says he is all right. He fainted from weakness more than anything.'

'Thank God!' said Paula with a deep sigh.

She took a letter from her pocket.

'May I trust you to give this to him from me?' she added.

Diana reddened as she took the letter.

'Yes. I'll give it to him.'

'And my travelling-case — if you would have it sent to the luggage office at Paddington, I will collect it there,' added Paula.

'I don't live in this house,' muttered Diana. 'But I'll give Lady Strange your message. I'm just going into the garden to tell them — about things.'

Paula bit her lower lip. Once she had loved Jack's mother — longed for Lady Strange to love her. But now all that was finished — and Lady Strange would think of her with horror and contempt — think the worst.

She drove away from 'The Whyspers' feeling as if she were in a particularly vivid nightmare. She had no idea where she was going or what she meant to do. She could think of nothing but Jack. But she remained calm and composed until she found herself alone in the compartment of an express from Marlborough to Paddington. Then she broke down and buried her face in her hands.

*   *   *

Everything and everybody seemed in chaos at 'The Whyspers' after Paula's departure.

When Jack recovered consciousness he demanded (as she had expected he would) to see Paula. The nurse told him that she was out and that he must lie quietly. She was not too pleased with her patient. He was still much too pale and weak. Obviously he had had a shock. Geraldine had intimated at some disturbance between him and his fiancée, who later had left the house. But the news must be broken to the patient gently.

Jack, weak though he was, however, had strength enough to insist on his orders being obeyed.

'I want to see Paula — at once!' he insisted weakly.

Flurried and worried, the nurse went downstairs where the family had gathered in the drawing-room. Diana was still with them, hugging secret satisfaction to herself, whilst pretending grief on their behalf. Sir James and Lady Strange had been told about Paula and Alan Rivers. Diana had repeated the conversation she had overheard in the garden. She had said enough to convince the family that Paula was unworthy of Jack's love.

Sir James looked deeply troubled and shocked. Lady Strange was weeping. Gerry marched up and down the room tossing her head.

'I don't see why we need waste any tears. She was a bad character — good thing we found out — lucky escape for poor old Jack!' she was saying.

The nurse interrupted by informing them that Jack insisted on seeing Paula.

The members of the family exchanged glances. Finally, Lady Strange said, handkerchief pressed to her redrimmed eyes: 'Diana dear, you know more than any of us — and you are an old friend of Jack's. Possibly he would resent your explanation of Paula's absence less than ours. You have a letter for him from her too, haven't you?'

'Yes,' said Diana, nodding her golden head. 'Shall I go up to him?'

'Do, my dear,' said Lady Strange.

Diana's heart leaped with triumph when she entered Jack's room and approached his bed. This was her hour. She meant to make the best of it.

Jack, moving restlessly on his pillows, stared at her.

'Diana!' he said in surprise.

'Yes, Jack,' she said in a low, sweet voice. 'I have come to talk to you.'

'It is kind of you, but I want Paula,' he said feverishly. 'I particularly want to see her. You don't understand what happened — '

'Yes, my dear, I do,' Diana broke in gently, drawing a chair up to his bedside. 'I know everything. I knew before you did.'

He stared up at her, his dark eyes burning.

'About what?'

'About Paula and Alan.'

Jack moistened his dry lips with his tongue.

'Diana, I can't discuss it with you. You don't know what I feel. He insulted Paula — his allegations were pretty grim — I tried to get to him, but I'm so damnably weak — I fainted. I must see her.'

'Paula is no longer here.'

Jack's heart missed a beat.

'What do you mean?' he gasped.

'She has gone, Jack — left 'The Whyspers' for good.'

He stared at the girl in amazement.

'Gone!' he broke out passionately. 'Who let her go? Who let her go — without seeing me first?'

'She went of her own accord,' said Diana glibly. 'And Alan — '

'Has gone with her?'

'I don't know. But I understand he has left Marlborough,' said Diana dishonestly.

Jack's face was twisted into a suffering mask. Drops of moisture rolled down his forehead.

'Diana,' he said, 'what does this all mean?'

She told him. She said that she had known for some time that Alan was a former lover of Paula's. She repeated the conversation she had heard between them in the garden — repeated it so cleverly that Paula was thoroughly incriminated. In so many words, she definitely stated that Paula had lived with Alan, as his wife, in Paris, and that Peter Westbury had known it — had been introduced to Paula as 'Mrs. Rivers' in Paris; that was why Peter had always treated Paula coldly.

Jack listened to all this in silence. Every word cut him like a knife — sank into his very soul. He remembered what he had seen in the lounge today — Alan holding Paula in his arms — reminding her that she belonged to him.

'Diana,' he said in a hoarse voice, 'do you swear you have told me the truth?'

'I swear it, Jack!'

'And she has gone — left no message for me?'

Diana gave him the letter Paula had written.

Weakly Jack tore open the envelope and scanned the note Paula had left for him.

'Jack, my darling, I know things will look black against me and that they will lead you to believe I am guilty. I was in Paris with Alan Rivers, but only for a few hours. I did not live with him. But he has let everybody believe I did and I cannot prove that I did not. I am going away because I can never, never marry you with such a shadow between us. But I will always love and adore you. I think my heart is absolutely broken. Forgive me for not telling you before about Alan. I was too frightened. I love you so. Goodbye, Jack. — Paula.'

He read the letter twice. When at length he raised his head, some of the anguish was erased from it. To him, every word she had written rang with sincerity. The pathos of those words — 'I was too frightened — I love you so — ' haunted him. Too frightened — of losing him, of losing his love — poor kid, poor, suffering Paula.

'Diana,' he said in a deep voice, 'Paula says she is innocent.'

'But you can't possibly believe that!'

'I do believe it,' said Jack quietly, folding the note and putting it under his pillow. 'And now my one wish is to get strong enough to find her and bring her back again.'

Diana rose. She was trembling with anger.

'You must be mad, Jack.'

'Perhaps,' he said with a short laugh. 'Apparently you don't know the meaning of love — of real love such as mine is for Paula — hers for me — '

'And supposing you find her — with the other man?'

Jack's face flushed, then grew pale. He looked with steady dark eyes up at the face of Diana Cotesmore.

'Then I shall come back, alone,' he said. 'But I am convinced I shall not find that. Have you Paula's address?'

'No,' said Diana. 'She left no address.'

'That will make things difficult, but I will find her,' said Jack. 'You can tell mother and the others what I say. Now

190

please leave me, Diana. I feel absolutely done in.'

She walked out of the room feeling infuriated.

But Jack turned his face to the pillow and crushed Paula's letter in his hand.

'My darling,' he murmured, 'I must get strong quickly and find you. I forgive you everything — I love you so much, how could I help forgiving you? Oh, Paula, why did you go? Why did you think my love could not stand a test like this?'

5

Paula stepped out of the train at Paddington, a forlorn figure, staring up and down the crowded platform. She looked pale and wretched, and her eyes were swollen from weeping. She stood there, clutching her suitcase and bag, trying to make up her mind where to go.

She dared not go home. Her family still believed she was disgraced and ought to be married to Alan. From them she would get no help or sympathy. She must earn her own living; go her own way in future. But she had come away in such a hurry, her mind was dazed, incapable of clear thought. And she realised suddenly that she was alone in London with only a few pounds in her possession. What could she do — without money?

Fear crept over her, chilling her. And

while she stood there hesitating, a tall man in grey, carrying a suitcase, was swinging down the platform towards her. The blood rushed to her face as she recognised Alan. As he reached her side she stepped back a pace.

'You — you have dared to follow me?' she choked.

'Of course. I watched you leave 'The Whyspers' and caught the same train, only we travelled in different carriages,' said Alan coolly. 'My dear girl, you have met with all this trouble through me. Did you think I'd let you face the world alone?'

Paula's eyes gleamed with anger and fear.

'You had no right to follow me. You've done me enough harm,' she said. 'Oh, leave me alone, or you will drive me mad!'

'Now listen, Paula,' he said, ignoring her request. 'You're in London with no money, I'm certain, and nowhere to go. Strange has finished with you. You can't marry him now, can you?'

'No,' she said, wincing. 'Thanks to you.'

'Well, then, be sensible and marry me,' he said. 'I've got plenty of money and you used to care for me once. You'll care for me again. Come, Paula, let me take you to a hotel and leave you there, and tomorrow we'll get married by special licence.'

She shuddered and looked at him with eyes of loathing.

'No, never. Go away. Leave me alone.'

'Come along,' he said quietly, taking her arm. 'Don't waste time fighting me. One day you will have to come to me. You might as well save a lot of trouble and come now.'

She shivered and turned from him.

'I'd rather starve than come to you for help.'

'You have no money — nowhere to go,' he said. 'Why be such a little fool? As my wife you'll have everything money can buy. I'll be good to you, Paula. I swear it.'

'Good to me?' She laughed bitterly. 'I don't want your goodness. And I prefer any privation or hardship to luxury at such a price. It makes me ill even to imagine myself in your arms.'

The man reddened angrily. He had colossal conceit — an inordinate confidence in his own personal charm. It was unpleasant to hear a girl reject his advances with such contempt, such hatred. But he wanted her — nothing would prevent him from taking her, in the end.

'Come,' he insisted. 'You must, Paula. You're finished with Strange and Marlborough. Put it all out of your mind and come with me.'

She shrank away from him.

'Oh, leave me alone,' she implored.

'I shall never leave you alone,' he said doggedly. 'Never, until you marry me.'

Paula pressed a hand to her forehead. The pain in her temples was so intense she felt sick, blind with it. After all the agony she had gone through — the anguish of parting from Jack and

195

bidding farewell to all her hopes of happiness with him, this persistent persecution from Alan was almost more than she could endure. She felt that she had neither the physical nor mental strength to bear it without breaking down.

'But I shall never give way to him,' she told herself. 'Never. He will never win — '

'Come, Paula,' he repeated. 'It's time we left the platform. People are staring.'

She allowed him to take her outside the station, where cabs rolled up and away, porters shouted and gesticulated, vans rattled, people hurried about purposefully. The noise made the pain in her head worse. Alan looked down at her pale, suffering face.

'Look here, Paula,' he said in a tone of contrition, 'don't look like that. It makes me feel such a brute, and — '

'What does that matter?' she broke in bitterly. 'You are a brute, but feeling it doesn't help you to do anything about it.'

'I want to marry you.'

'I love Jack Strange and I hate you.'

He sighed. 'How obstinate you can be! Oh, well, I'm going to be patient. I know you'll come to me in the end.'

'If you worry me much longer you'll drive me insane,' she said, now on the verge of nervous hysteria. 'Then you can have me — senseless, witless — if you like. I shouldn't care.'

'You want a stiff brandy and soda and a good night's rest,' he said calmly.

'What a horror you are!' she said in a low tone.

'Taxi!' called Alan to a porter, ignoring this speech.

Paula's heart began to race. She felt genuinely afraid of Alan now. She was not going to be bullied into accompanying him to a hotel. She would not go with him.

The taxi drew up. Alan took her arm.

'After you,' he said.

'No,' said Paula in a smothered voice. 'You have no right — no right at all — I want to go my own way — oh, for heaven's sake — '

Her voice was drowned in the blare of a motor-horn. She felt dizzy, weak with protesting and arguing. Alan literally pushed her into the taxi. She found herself in it, driving out of Paddington Station towards the West End.

He gave a grim smile and touched her knee.

'No use fighting me, Paula,' he said. 'You've just got to give in.'

She shrank as far from him as she could get in her corner of the taxi, one hand pressed to her burning forehead. If she had felt well, strong physically, she could have fought him with greater resistance. But all she had been through and lack of nourishment had made her wretchedly weak and incapable of asserting herself.

'Oh, let me alone,' she moaned. 'Can't you see that I don't want to marry you? I won't! I won't!'

'Yes you will,' he said coolly, lighting a cigarette.

She stared at him with eyes that seemed blurred.

'When this taxi stops I shall get out and leave you,' she said in a hoarse voice. 'I'm going my own way — you shan't stop me, you devil!'

'Come, come, Paula,' he laughed, 'don't lose your temper. Now honestly, where can you go and what can you do? You've no money, beyond a pound or two in your purse, and no job. Your own family won't have you, and Lady Strange won't give you a reference after what has happened. You'll be better off in my care, I assure you.'

Paula tried to speak, to argue, but no words came. The buzzing, the pain in her head was growing worse. She felt desperately ill now, and really frightened.

She heard Alan's voice from far, far off.

'What's the matter, Paula? Feeling odd?'

He was anxious now. She looked ghastly pale and her eyelids were closing. He took the seat beside her and put an arm around her shoulders.

She was dimly conscious of his arm about her — his handsome face bending over her. She made a feeble effort to speak, to protest. Then she lost consciousness.

Alan felt the slim body sag, and the small head fell forward on his chest. He realised that she had fainted. It had all been too much for her. And it was no ordinary faint. She was ill, obviously. Perhaps her brain had been affected by the shock of recent events.

Alan's heart beat quickly and he bit his lip as he stared down at the pale face of the insensible girl. The fact that she was helpless now, unable to defend herself, roused no chivalry in him. He only realised with mounting excitement that she was absolutely in his power.

By the time the taxi had reached the hotel in Piccadilly he had formed a clever plan.

He assumed an expression of grave anxiety as the smart commissionaire opened the taxi door.

'My wife is ill — has fainted,' he said briefly. 'Help me carry her into the hotel. We have come from Paddington and were intending to stay in town a few days.'

The man was all respectful concern; Paula was very light — much too thin and light. She was soon carried out of the taxi through the lounge, past a crowd of curious people, into the passenger lift.

Alan booked an expensive suite of rooms, and signed the register 'Mr. and Mrs. Alan Rivers — Marlborough.' A few minutes later he was standing in the luxurious sitting-room of his suite giving instructions to the maid for whom he had rung.

'My wife is rather delicate and subject to bad fainting fits. Will you look after her for a bit?' he said. 'I have asked the porter to send for a doctor.'

The maid hurried into the adjoining bedroom. Paula looked like a child, her small head sunk in the pillows, her eyes closed.

Alan coolly walked into the room. He behaved like any anxious, dutiful husband. The maid thought him most handsome and charming. Madame was fortunate to be married to such a pleasant gentleman.

Brandy had little effect upon Paula. She stirred, choked, moaned a little, then lay still again. She was certainly in no slight faint.

Alan began to grow nervous. He was relieved when the doctor arrived. By that time the maid had undressed Paula and got her into bed. Alan had half unpacked his things in his own bedroom, which led out of Paula's.

Alan lied easily and smoothly to the doctor.

His wife was not at all strong — had found the train journey from Marlborough trying — was easily overcome by heat — had been dazed, wandering in her mind for some days — he was horribly worried.

The doctor gave him a few encouraging words and made an examination of Paula. She seemed particularly young and slender and pathetically childish to be a married woman. But naturally he did not for an instant doubt that she was Mrs. Rivers. In the taxi Alan had slid a platinum wedding ring on Paula's marriage finger. He was a man of experience and the ring travelled with him.

The verdict of the physician was 'a bad nervous breakdown,' due to great mental strain or shock. Mrs. Rivers would probably recover consciousness fairly soon, but be very weak, very ill. She must have the utmost care and quiet, and would need a hospital nurse.

Alan — the epitome of an anxious husband — sat by Paula's bedside waiting for her to wake. He must be there, he reflected, to tell her what he had done. It seemed to him that in the circumstances she would have no choice but to give in to him. Fate had literally pushed her into his arms.

It was late that night when Paula opened her eyes. Perplexedly she stared around the big, beautiful bedroom — then at two figures — one hatefully familiar — that tall, fair-haired man — the other a strange hospital nurse in a spotless white apron and veil.

She lifted a hand to her head. She felt remarkably weak and feeble, and when she spoke it was in a whisper.

'Alan — '

She spoke the name of the man because she knew him — because she was terrified and dazed and did not know where she was or what had happened.

Alan at once left the nurse's side and came to her, knelt down and took her hands, his heart racing.

'Paula — oh, my darling — you are awake at last!' he said loudly for the nurse's benefit. Then he whispered rapidly against her ear: 'Listen, Paula — don't make a fuss — you fainted in the taxi — I brought you here up to this suite as my wife — the doctor has seen you — everybody thinks you're Mrs. Rivers — take my advice and don't undeceive them and cause a fuss and scandal, otherwise it will get into the papers and Jack Strange will see it.'

Weak, ill though she felt, Paula comprehended quite clearly all that he said. She grew more frightened, felt more helpless than ever. But she said nothing. What could she do? He had taken full advantage of her collapse. She was here in this hotel as his wife — she saw the strange wedding-ring on her finger. He had won — at least for the time being, until she was well enough to get away from him. Sick despair settled over her.

'You'll soon be all right, darling,' he said, stroking her hair (still for the benefit of the nurse), and against her ear, on pretence of kissing her cheek: 'Don't worry, Paula. Just lie quiet and get better. I swear I'll marry you as soon as you'll agree to it, and I won't touch a hair of your head until you are really my wife.'

She shuddered.

'Jack,' she inwardly cried. 'Jack — what would you say if you knew? Oh, it isn't my fault — I tried so hard to fight — '

She was too ill and tired to fight any more.

★ ★ ★

So long as Paula was really ill, Alan was comparatively kind and sincerely anxious on her behalf. But after a week, when she was growing stronger and declaring her intention of getting up and sending the nurse away, he showed himself for what he really was.

He was quite aware that this position tortured and distressed Paula — that she had hated being confined to this hotel bedroom as Mrs. Alan Rivers. But it amused him considerably, and he felt confident that Paula would have no alternative now but to marry him.

Paula said little, but all the time she lay there in the big luxurious bed, surrounded by all the comforts money could buy, she was silently awaiting the hour when she could get up and leave Alan for ever.

'I was ill and weak when I left 'The Whyspers',' she told herself. 'But I shan't faint or give in again — next time I make up my mind to escape Alan I shall succeed.'

Her one desire now was to get well. She obeyed the doctor who attended her; ate the nourishing foods given her; tried to remain quiet and not to give way to anxious or anguished thought. Whenever she remembered Jack her pain was almost unendurable. She wondered how he had taken the news of her departure — what he thought of her. She prayed he did not think too badly. She loved him so. She would never, never forget the beauty, the sweetness of their love. As for really becoming the wife of Alan Rivers — the mere thought revolted her.

Whenever Alan entered her bedroom her small face grew rigid — her eyes dark with hatred. He knew just how she felt about him. So now, when she was stronger, he took pleasure in tormenting her, knowing she dared not repulse him.

One afternoon he came and sat on the edge of her bed. The nurse was in attendance, she thought Paula a fortunate girl to possess so delightful a husband. The bedroom was full of flowers — great dewy roses, huge masses of lilac, hot-house carnations — all from Alan. On the table beside her stood a bowl of fruit — an expensive box of French chocolates — a pile of the latest illustrated magazines — some new novels. What more could a husband buy for his wife? The nurse was rather nettled with Paula for being so cool, so silent, so seemingly ungrateful to her young husband.

Alan, with a charming smile on his handsome face, played with Paula's hands, quite aware that she shivered from the contact with him.

'You're much better, aren't you,

darling?' he murmured. 'Tomorrow nurse thinks you'll be able to get up, and the day after, if it keeps fine, you shall come out for a drive in the park.'

Paula's eyes narrowed. She said nothing, but silently decided that if she was strong enough to go out for a drive, she would be strong enough to get out unnoticed, take a taxi and escape from this man altogether.

'How adorable you look in your new jacket, Paula,' Alan observed.

Her heart beat with anger, with futile scorn of him. How she hated him — hated the presents he had showered on her. Never could she forgive him for this shabby trick he had played on her.

Her face was pale and thin in its frame of copper hair, but she looked lovely — lovely enough to fascinate any man. Alan's heart missed a beat as he looked down at her. Everybody believed her to be his wife — his wife —

'You're beautiful,' he said, bending over her.

She shivered uncontrollably.

'Please!' she protested under her breath. 'Please leave my room, Alan.'

But he lost his head. Suddenly his arms went round her; he crushed her lips in a searing kiss.

The nurse discreetly tip-toed out of the room.

For a moment, in tense silence, Paula fought with him. Her heart beat with suffocating speed. She was terrified. Madly she struggled in his arms, fought to evade his burning kisses.

'Let me go!' she gasped, her eyes brilliant with tears of sheer rage. 'Let me go, I say — '

He buried his face against her soft throat.

'My wife,' he said with a mocking smile.

It was more than Paula could bear.

'Nurse! Nurse!' she called out.

The woman came hurrying in. Alan sprang up from the bed and walked to the window, his face crimson. Paula held out a trembling hand to the nurse.

'I — feel — faint,' she gasped. 'I

— I'm afraid I scared — my husband.'

Alan's lips curled into a faint smile.

She had got the better of him this time. Well, she would see. He would win her in the end. He walked out of the room, jammed a hat fiercely on his head and marched from the hotel.

The nurse, thinking 'Mrs. Rivers' had been overexcited, tucked her up, drew the curtains and bade her sleep until tea-time.

Paula lay still on her pillows, her eyes shut.

'Oh, Jack, Jack, I want you so,' she inwardly groaned.

She was growing terrified of Alan. Tomorrow she would get away — somehow.

Next morning, Alan had to go out on business. He announced his intention of returning at midday to take Paula for a drive. It was a brilliant summer morning, and the doctor said the fresh air would do her good.

Paula resorted to cunning in her desperate desire to escape Alan.

'I'd like to go out alone with my — my husband,' she murmured to the nurse. 'You go out a bit yourself, nurse, and when Alan returns he'll find me alone waiting for him.'

The nurse thought that a pretty idea. She dressed her patient, wrapped her in a mink coat (recently purchased by Alan) and left her.

As soon as the woman had gone, Paula went to the wardrobe — pulled out her own coat and skirt and re-dressed herself. With loathing she flung the mink away from her. Then, in mad haste, before he should return, she packed the suitcase and prepared to run away. She felt horribly weak and her hands trembled as she moved. But she was much better — well enough to get away, she told herself. Get away she must.

Her heart raced with mingled fright and excitement as she stole out into the corridor and down in the lift. She was terrified lest Alan should meet her. But the coast was clear. In another moment she was in a taxi, with her own modest belongings and a few pounds in her bag, bound for a cheap private hotel in Bloomsbury of which she knew.

It must have been exactly five minutes later that another taxi rolled up to the hotel Paula had just left, and a tall, thin, good-looking man with dark eyes and hair and his left arm in a sling, got out and walked into the vestibule.

It was Jack Strange.

Jack, too, had escaped from doctors and nurses and deliberately come up to London to find the girl he loved and in whom he still believed.

He was by no means strong. His face looked pale and weary and he had lost all his old buoyancy and strength. But he walked firmly to the desk to book his room. It was by a strange coincidence that he had chosen this very hotel. But it was one of the most comfortable in town and he had been here before. He had no notion where Paula was, but he knew she was in London; that her luggage had been sent from 'The

Whyspers' to Paddington. He was determined to engage the services of the best detective in London to trace her, if need be. He loved her. He wanted her. The chagrin and anger of the family did not matter to him. Nothing mattered — except Paula.

Signing the register, he ran his gaze idly down the list of names. And suddenly his heart gave a great bound. He had seen the entry — Mr. and Mrs. Alan Rivers.

As Jack stared blindly at that damning piece of evidence, his haggard young face grew pale, and for a moment he felt not merely misery, but hot rage in his heart. Rage against Alan for taking the woman he loved and wanted for his wife — anger against Paula for being false. He had trusted her absolutely. He felt the most passionate resentment against her for breaking his faith, breaking his heart.

So everything they had insinuated at home was not without foundation. Everything Diana had said about Paula was true. She had just played with him — and had left him for a former lover.

The anger died down in Jack. It was replaced by a strange disbelief — a strange feeling that it was not the Paula he had loved and trusted who had let him down like this. He began to question the reception clerk.

'I see some friends of mine — Mr. and Mrs. Rivers — are here. When did they come?'

'Eight or nine days ago.'

'Do you know — Mrs. Rivers well by sight? Could you — describe her to me?'

The reception clerk glanced curiously at Jack.

'Yes,' she said. 'Mrs. Rivers came to the hotel in rather a dramatic fashion. She was carried in from a taxi unconscious.'

Jack's heart leaped. His eyes dilated with sudden excitement.

'Unconscious? Why? What was the matter?'

'She was very ill — had fainted in the

taxi, I was told. She was carried up to her room by her husband and a porter.

'Yes, yes,' said Jack, his lips dry, his heart racing. 'That is the Mrs. Rivers I know. But when was this?'

The clerk told him the exact date and time. Jack pieced the bits of information together. He deduced that Paula must have come up from Marlborough almost immediately after he had discovered her with Alan that day and had fainted on the stairs. From the time it appeared she must have come straight to the hotel from Paddington. How, then, could she be married to Rivers — unless she was married before? But that was incredible, impossible.

Wild thoughts chased through Jack's brain. Paula — for Paula it must be, from the clerk's description — had been taken up to the suite booked by Alan, insensible, and had been in bed ever since. She was up there now, ill. Perhaps she had been drugged — perhaps this had all been done against her will.

'What is the number of the Rivers' suite?' he asked the clerk. 'I'd like to go up — to see Mrs. Rivers.'

'One moment,' said the girl laconically, 'I'll ring. What name shall I say?'

'Mr. Strange.'

Another few moments and Paula's absence from her bedroom and the hotel was discovered. The reception clerk shrugged her shoulders.

'I don't know where she is, I'm sure,' she said in answer to Jack's anxious inquiries. 'I thought she was still in bed. Mr. Rivers is out, so is the hospital nurse in attendance.'

Jack's brain seethed. Every moment he grew more and more certain that there was something queer about this — that Paula had been brought here and detained against her will. Yes, he was certain of it. And if she had run away today, he would find her.

He rushed through the lounge to the hall-porter — shot a few rapid questions at him. The man answered with intelligence. Yes, he had seen a lady he thought to be Mrs. Rivers come out this morning, carrying a suitcase. He had called a taxi for her.

'Well — did you hear her give the driver an address?' demanded Jack.

'I did, sir, but I forget — '

'Try to remember,' interrupted Jack. He slid a ten-shilling note into the man's hand.

The porter's eyes beamed. He broke into a smile and scratched his head.

'I think the lady said 24 or 34 Coheren Street, Bloomsbury. Wait a bit, sir — or was it an 'otel — yes, it was — the Coherne Hotel, Bloomsbury.'

Jack's pulses raced with excitement. Anger, misery, these sensations had died within him, save the feeling that he was on the track of a great discovery — that at the Coherne Hotel, wherever that was, he would find Paula and make her explain.

At that precise moment, as he stood on the steps of the hotel talking to the hall-porter, a beautiful burgundy-coloured touring car rolled noiselessly up to the entrance. Jack glanced at it idly at first. Then his face grew set and he stiffened in every limb. Out of that car stepped a tall, fair man with a soft hat at a jaunty angle on his head, and a cigarette between his lips — Alan Rivers.

Jack was feeling none too strong for an encounter of this kind, but he plunged into it in his hot-headed way. He regarded Rivers with suspicion and dislike. He did not mean to miss this opportunity of facing him.

Alan was both amazed and dismayed to see Jack Strange at the hotel, but he greeted him nonchalantly.

'Hullo, Strange. What are you doing up in town?'

Jack walked up to him and met his gaze levelly.

'I've come up to find Paula,' he said.

Alan put his tongue in his cheek. 'Well?' he drawled. 'She's my wife.'

'I'm not sure of that,' said Jack tersely. 'At any rate, I have to prove it yet.'

'My dear fellow — Paula is very ill and up in her bedroom — ' began Alan.

'That is where you are wrong,' broke in Jack with a feeling of satisfaction. 'Paula is not in the hotel.'

Alan's face changed colour.

'Then where is she?'

'At an hotel in Bloomsbury. I know the address. It is all distinctly odd, Rivers. Why should your wife — if she is your wife — take advantage of your absence to leave the hotel with her luggage? It looks to me as though she was forced here against her will.'

Alan bit his lip. He felt suddenly furious and chagrined that Paula had escaped from him.

'Oh, damn it all!' he said violently. 'I'm getting sick of Paula — and of you!'

Jack's hand shot out and gripped his arm.

'Not so fast, Rivers. You're coming with me.'

'Oh, am I?' sneered Alan. 'And where?'

'To Paula. You are going to face her in front of me and explain all this,' said Jack through clenched teeth. 'There is too much mystery about it all. I don't believe Paula is married to you, and I don't believe she cares an ounce for you. You've got some hold over her, no doubt, which made her leave Marlborough and me, but you're going to explain it all, or — by heaven! — you'll pay for it.'

Alan opened his lips as though to speak, then shut them again. He shot Jack a vicious look. But he was yellow as well as a moral blackguard, and he saw that Jack meant what he said. He had only one free arm, but he could probably use that one fist to advantage — and would. Alan sized up his man pretty well. He imagined he had won Paula; had thought himself on the point of persuading her. But Paula had gone and Strange had found her. Well, what use to pursue her any longer? He was genuinely sick of it all. He had money, looks, position — why throw himself away on a woman who hated him and whined all day for another man? He had been a fool — a stubborn fool — ever to set his heart on getting Paula.

'Well?' rapped out Jack. 'What have you to say?'

'Nothing much,' said Alan, with a short laugh, 'except that you've won, Strange, and I'm too sick of the whole business to worry about it any further.'

'I see. Then will you please explain — or come with me now to Paula — '

'I'm not coming,' said Alan savagely. 'I don't want any more scenes. You've won — Paula's won. She isn't my wife.'

'Ah!' said Jack under his breath.

'She fainted in the taxi coming with me from Paddington,' continued Alan sullenly. 'I had her taken into the hotel as my wife, and nursed back to health. But I did her no harm. She's just as innocent as the day she left Marlborough.'

Jack drew a deep breath.

'Go on,' he said tersely. 'And what about Paris? The truth, mind you,

Rivers, and nothing but the truth.'

'She eloped with me to Paris,' said Alan, shrugging his shoulders. 'But she didn't live with me. She ran away from me. I don't believe she ever really cared for me. At any rate, she's all you believe her to be, and I've been a fool. Now do you want any more?'

Jack released his arm.

'No. I want no more. I can only say that if any man deserves to be thrashed publicly, you do.'

Alan gave a short, angry laugh. He was furiously angry, furious because he was defeated and thwarted. 'Anyhow, I'm going to clear out. I've had enough of women. Marry Paula and be happy.'

If Jack had felt stronger and better he would have hit Alan Rivers there and then. But as it was, he felt giddy and weak and at the back of his mind danced the glorious, relieving thought that Paula was innocent — that there was nothing now between them — no shadow of doubt — no ugly suspicion.

He stumbled down the steps and hailed a passing taxi.

* * *

When Jack Strange marched into the Bloomsbury Hotel where Paula had fled for refuge, and inquired for her, he was told she was in her room.

'The young lady arrived rather weak and tired — has been very ill,' the manageress informed Jack. 'I believe she's resting. Shall I tell her you're here?'

'No — I'll go up to her,' said Jack recklessly. 'I'm her husband.'

He delighted in the lie. He was radiantly happy at the thought that he had found her — that he could tell her everything was all right.

The manageress gave a shocked exclamation.

'Her husband? But she's calling herself Miss Broughton!'

Jack threw the woman one of his irresistible, boyish smiles.

'To tell the truth, she's run away from me,' he said. 'But I'm going to take her home again right now.'

'Dear me!' said the manageress, thrilled. 'Fancy that, now.'

Two minutes later, Jack was knocking on the door of No. 25. Paula's voice said 'Come in.' And he walked straight in.

Paula felt wretchedly weak after her exciting escape from Alan, but she had made up her mind that on the morrow she must look for a job. When Jack entered she was examining the 'Situation Vacant' column of several daily papers. Jack thought he had never seen a more pathetic sight. Such a pale, forlorn little figure with ruffled hair and sad eyes much too shadowy and sorrowful for that delicate face.

She stared at Jack, surprised and incredulous. The shock of seeing him made her speechless — almost stunned. Then she gave a low cry.

'Jack — you!'

'Paula,' he said. 'Oh, my poor Paula!'

And the next moment his arm was round her, holding her close, close to his heart. His warm, swift kisses fell on her cheeks, her hair, her eyes.

'Paula, my darling, my life, my love — '

She clung to him mutely, with passionate relief and delight. She shut her eyes and surrendered to his kisses, wishing she might die before she awakened and found it was all a dream.

But when at last he raised his head and she could open her eyes and look at him, she knew he was indeed real — his warm, living presence was there beside her.

'Jack, Jack!' she cried. 'Oh, how did you find me? Why have you come?'

He told her in a few brief words — explained how he had come up to London to look for her and how fate had led him to the very hotel where she had stayed. He described the meeting with Alan and his confession.

'I know you are innocent — that he was a liar,' he finished. 'I always believed in you, Paula, from the beginning.'

She laid her head on his shoulders and began to cry — tears of sheer weakness and rapturous relief.

'I couldn't have stayed — have let you marry me while Alan lied about Paris,' she sobbed. 'That's why I ran away. But oh, Jack, my dear, I'm so thankful he has owned up at last.'

'My poor Paula! How you must have suffered!' said Jack, his lips on her hair. 'Now you must rest and get well, and tomorrow I shall take you home with me again.'

'No, no — not back there, Jack. They all hate me and distrust me.'

'I shall tell them exactly what Rivers has said.'

'Must I go back there, Jack?'

'Why, no, darling. We'll get married by special licence and go straight down to Cornwall and let the sea air bring us both back to life. We're a couple of weak, foolish people and we want rest and quiet, eh, darling?'

He gave a happy laugh.

'And, Paula,' he went on, 'you must promise never, never to run away from me again!'

She looked up at him, her eyes full of love and happiness.

'I shall never want to, Jack. Although' — with a smile — 'it's nice to be found again.'

We do hope that you have enjoyed reading this large print book.

Did you know that all of our titles are available for purchase?

We publish a wide range of high quality large print books including:
Romances, Mysteries, Classics
General Fiction
Non Fiction and Westerns

Special interest titles available in large print are:
The Little Oxford Dictionary
Music Book, Song Book
Hymn Book, Service Book

Also available from us courtesy of Oxford University Press:
Young Readers' Dictionary
(large print edition)
Young Readers' Thesaurus
(large print edition)

For further information or a free brochure, please contact us at:
Ulverscroft Large Print Books Ltd.,
The Green, Bradgate Road, Anstey,
Leicester, LE7 7FU, England.
Tel: (00 44) **0116 236 4325**
Fax: (00 44) **0116 234 0205**

When Jenna Maitland's cousin Joss flees the responsibilities of their family's department store empire in Yorkshire, he escapes to Cornwall to follow his true calling and paint. Accompanied by the mysterious Gil Ryder, Jenna sets off south to find him. Once in Cornwall, Jenna finds herself becoming increasingly attracted to Gil — but is warned off by the attractive Victoria Symington, who appears to regard Gil as her own. Meanwhile, Joss's whereabouts has been discovered — but he is refusing to return . . .

BROKEN PROMISES

Chrissie Loveday

The greatest day of Carolyn's life has arrived: she is to marry her beloved Henry. But when she gets to the church, it becomes clear that something is terribly wrong. The groom has disappeared! Devastated, Carolyn is supported by her brother and his girlfriend as she tries to pick up the pieces of her life. When she meets kind, caring Jed, she feels as if she really is over Henry — but is this just a rebound? And will she ever find out why she was jilted at the altar?

HER HIGHLAND LAIRD

Carol MacLean

Fleeing her unfaithful fiancé, Lara sticks a pin in the map and vows to go wherever it lands. She finds herself in the cool summer of the Scottish Highlands, landing a job at Invermalloch Estate. Here, she meets Cal, the brooding Laird who is hiding from his own painful past. A powerful attraction between them slowly turns to love. But when Cal is called back to America, will this love survive — or will Lara's Highland Laird prove to be only a summer romance?

BIG GIRLS DON'T CRY

Sally Quilford

It is 1962, and WPC Bobbie Bland-ford is in her third year at Stony End station. Her relationship with boyfriend Dr Leo Stanhope is decidedly rocky, and she faces a continuing struggle to earn the same respect that is paid to her male colleagues. When a violent bank robbery shocks the entire village, Bobbie's talented — but seemingly troubled — brother Tom arrives from Scotland Yard, placing her on the sidelines of the investigation. Can Bobbie find out the truth, resolve things with Leo, and stop her brother from ruining his career?

LOVE AND LIES

Pamela Fudge

When Dana Abraham agrees to look after her friend's secretarial agency, she must deal with Alexander Mitchell, who has rejected every woman the agency has sent: the prettier they are, the meaner he is. Dana decides to fulfil the role of perfect secretary herself, and goes in a frumpy disguise to win him over. But Mr Mean-and-Moody Mitchell is not the bully she expects, and she finds herself becoming attracted to him. It seems he has growing feelings for her, too — but will they last when he discovers her deception?